Twits in Peril

A Steampunk Distraction

Tom Alan Robbins

Book Two of THE TWITS CHRONICLES

Claim A Free Gift!

Visit Twitschronicles.com to claim a free copy of the Twits short story *Uncle Hugo's Crisis"*. Or, if you are reading this on a device, you can click HERE.

What People Are Saying:

"The Twits Chronicles are hilarious, blessed with truly exceptional dialogue. Steampunk dystopia meets Oscar Wildean wit in these books. I found myself laughing out loud on numerous occasions--and that's not something I often do while reading. " —**Nick Sullivan**, author of The Deep Series and *Zombie Bigfoot*.

"Delightful! A frothy frappe of P.G. Wodehouse and steam-punk. If you're the sort who reads blurbs before reading the book, stop it. Stop it right now. Read TWITS IN LOVE and have a good time. These days we can all use a bit more of a good time." —**John Ostrander**, American writer of comic books, including *Suicide Squad*, *Grimjack* and *Star Wars: Legacy*.

"I haven't enjoyed the company of such eccentric characters since A Confederacy of Dunces, and Tom Alan Robbins has managed to place them in the stylized world of Oscar Wilde. A really unique journey." — **Kevin Conroy**, Actor, The voice behind the DC Comics superhero Batman .

"Tom Alan Robbins' Twits stories are hilarious, thought provoking and mind bending. His juicy turns of phrase will stick in your ear like a catchy song." — **Michael Urie**, Actor, Producer and Director

"Tom is the most talented, delicious writer. Do yourself a favor, and immerse yourself in the

fabulous world of TWITS!" — **Mary Testa**, 3
time Tony Award Nominee

The Author makes no representation of any kind as to his being a citizen of the United Kingdom, either native or naturalized. He is from a small town in Ohio, for which he apologizes.

This is a work of fiction. All events described are imaginary; all characters are entirely fictitious and are not intended to represent actual living persons.

Cover design by Melody J. Barber of Aurora Publicity

Additional designs by Eric Wright of The Puppet Kitchen.

Twits Logo designed by Feppa Rodriquez

Proofreading by Gretchen Tannert Douglas

To the members of Lab405 who gave freely the gold of their opinions and made me the writer that I am

Steampunk

"Steampunk is a subgenre of science fiction that incorporates retrofuturistic technology and aesthetics inspired by 19th-century industrial steam-powered machinery. Steampunk works are often set in an alternative history of the Victorian era or the American "Wild West", where steam power remains in mainstream use, or in a fantasy world that similarly employs steam power."

Wikipedia

A Word About Timelines

For those who are unfamiliar with the Steampunk genre, a word about timelines may be helpful. The Steampunk Universe in which The Twits Chronicles take place is clearly not our own. That is why events and cultural references that happened in vastly different eras in our own world seem to happen in a compressed time period. It feels as if we are in a vaguely Victorian era, and yet there are references to events and quotations from well into the twentieth century.

It may help to think of this as an exercise in "what if?" What if electricity wasn't discovered until much later in human history? Human ingenuity would still search for new ways of using existing technology, and so steam power and mechanical engineering would keep advancing, while much of the aesthetic of the world around us could remain in the nineteenth century.

The world that would result is the world of *The Twits Chronicles*. Other writers would use these same criteria to create very different realities. This is mine.

Enter and enjoy.

Contents

CHAPTER ONE

An Ill-Advised Wager

When the world is too much with us; when even the strongest anti-depressants have lost their power to soothe; when the music of life is drowned out by the rough chants of striking postal workers—one can always depend upon one's club. As I waited for my cocktail, I gazed at the brass and Naugahyde, whose patina derived from centuries of careful polishing by the staff—some of whom were as old as the club itself. Sven the bartender, for example, had been lovingly patched and repaired since my great-great-grandfather's day. He could remember when steak and kidney pie contained actual steak and kidneys. It must have been a savage time—members feasting on the organs of slaughtered animals. Now, of course, the animals are gone, along with the fish in the sea and the birds of the air, but Twits, my beloved club, remains.

Sven set a tumbler before me with two fingers of amber perfection sloshing from side to side. I stared at it gloomily. It was perfect yesterday, perfect today... it would be perfect tomorrow. Where was the spice of life to be found?

"Your brandy and Paxil, Sir."

"Thank you, Sven. Has Mr. Wickford-Davies been in today?"

"Not yet, Sir."

I raised the glass and gazed at the play of light shining through it.

There was a sudden flurry and a nasal bray from the doorway. "A moment, if you please, Mr. Chippington-Smythe!"

I turned to see the club's beady-eyed Marshall, Cubby Martinez cruising toward me like a uni-browed shark. If anyone could be described as my nemesis, it was he. I don't know from whence Cubby's animus derived. I suppose there was something in my scent that aggravated a primal instinct within him. He gripped a yardstick in his hairy paws.

"I'll just check those heels if I may."

I extended my feet. "Measure away, Cubby. You won't find any irregularities here. Not with Bentley on the job."

He snapped the yardstick next to my shoes and crouched down to peer at the number.

"Satisfied?"

He frowned at the yardstick. "I suppose it meets the requirements... barely, but if you get any wear on the rubber tips you'll be in violation."

I tossed my drink down the old sluice and waved a flipper at him. "When that day comes, Cubby my lad, there will be fruity pops in Hell."

He sniffed. "Just doing my job."

"Is it my imagination or are your eyes growing closer together? I ask merely for information."

Cubby's retort was lost in the sudden hubbub as a couple of old chums came rolling up to the bar. Ford and Lincoln had been my accomplices in many a schoolboy caper.

"Cyril, Old Shoe! Death before dishonour."

"Hallo, Ford. Hallo, Lincoln. Death before dishonour."

Ford peered at me with concern. "How goes the struggle?"

"You're looking rather hipped," observed Lincoln.

"Yes, I've got a touch of the Blue Meanies, I'm afraid."

"Here, Sven, a round of Brandy and Prozacs here. You just chug that down. That'll put you right."

Ford turned to Cubby, who was still gripping his yardstick. "Hallo, Cubby."

"Sir."

"Why don't you stick that yardstick somewhere inappropriate?"

Cubby reddened slightly. "Just enforcing the dress code."

"Fending off the barbarous hordes, eh? Carry on."

Lincoln sipped at his B and P and looked at me. "What've you got to be blue about? Riches beyond compare, young, bachelor. You ought to be kicking up your heels. Seems rather ungrateful of you."

"Money isn't everything," I muttered gloomily.

"It's a lot, though."

"I don't know. Sometimes I think the economically disadvantaged are happier than we. Their lives are so simple."

Lincoln screwed up his forehead. "I don't think that's true, Old Fish."

"It *is* true. They get food, shelter and hydrogen for free. They don't suffer under the cruel lash of fashion. I've seen them wearing shorts and flip-flops. Flip-flops! A far cry from the six-inch heels we're tottering around in this month."

Lincoln admired his calves. "You must admit they make your legs look fabulous!"

I sighed and stared down into my glass. "I dream sometimes of what it must be like to live as they do."

That got a hearty laugh from Ford. "You wouldn't last a day."

"Of course I would! A gentleman can fit in anywhere."

He gave a hoot and kicked back on his stool. "What'll you bet?"

"Seriously?"

Lincoln set down his tumbler. "Say, I'm in. I'll bet you can't live like the huddled masses for... let's say a week. Loser pays the winners' bar tab for a year."

Those who know me will tell you I have a weakness for gambling. My valet, Bentley, has often had to speak to me about it. Bentley, however was at home. It is difficult not to blame him for what followed. He usually has a kind of instinct that warns him when I'm about to get into trouble so that he can swoop in to save the day, but even if he had set out from home at the first mention of the bet, he wouldn't have arrived at the club in time to save me.

"You're on!"

Ford grabbed my hand and gave it a pump. "Hey, Cubby!"

"Sir?"

"Did you hear the bet?"

Cubby's eyes gleamed with ill will like a pug dog glaring from under a chaise. "Yes, Sir."

"Good. You're our witness. When does it start?"

I casually took a sip of my drink. "What about tomorrow morning?"

"Fine. Tomorrow morning."

I spied my cousin, Cheswick Wickford-Davies (Binky to his friends) tottering towards us, his stilettos clicking on the marble tiles.

"Hallo, chaps. What are you all conspiring about? Death before dishonour."

"Death before dishonour."

"Death before dishonour."

"Death, etc."

"We've just bet Cyril here that he can't last one week living like an ordinary citizen. Loser pays the winners' bar tab for a year."

Binky is almost as bad as I am when it comes to wagering, but unlike me he is almost always broke. He staggered a little as his heels slipped and grabbed at a stool for support. "Say, let me get in on this. I'll back Cyril for half his share."

Lincoln slapped the bar. "Done. Cubby?"

A smile played about the corners of Cubby's cruel mouth. "I've made a note, Sir."

Ford raised a finger. "And no help from Bentley."

This snapped me to attention. "What?"

"You go alone. Bentley must stay at home."

Terror gripped at my vitals. "Now wait a minute..."

Binky's voice was rather higher than usual. "That does change the complexion..."

"Cubby?"

The smile was growing more predatory. "Members of the general public are rarely attended by a valet."

"Blast! What a dreary week this is going to be."

Binky eyed me anxiously. "But you can do it, can't you? I mean, I've gone out on rather a limb."

"Nobody forced you to bet."

"Look here... bar tab for a year! These two drink like dipso-maniacal fishes.

I looked down my nose at him. "Fine! I said I could do it and I'll be damned if I show the white feather. How hard can it be?"

"That's the spirit. Let's go to your place and get you honed up."

Ford lifted his finger a second time. "And no fair telling the people you meet that you're rich."

Lincoln leaned in. "Yes. They'll fall all over themselves to help you if they think you'll come back later and shower them with gold."

"If they find out you're rich you lose."

I turned reluctantly to the Club Marshall, who was now grinning like a jack-o'-lantern.

"Cubby?"

"Sven, play back the wording of the bet."

Sven opened his mouth and Ford's voice issued forth in a perfect imitation. "I'll bet you can't live like the huddled masses for... let's say a week. Loser pays the winners' bar tab for a year."

Cubby tried unsuccessfully to look solicitous. "There you are, Sir. It is not enough to simply live among them. You must live *like* them. That means they must believe that you're one of them."

I shook my head vigorously. "I've changed my mind. No bet."

"Too late, Sir," Cubby intoned solemnly.

"Damn!"

"You could forfeit now."

"Never!" I glared at him. "You're enjoying this a tad too much, Cubby."

He stepped in close enough for me to smell the Impossible Mutton on his breath. "As Club Marshall I am impartial. As a private citizen may I say that I find the prospect of your impending humiliation delightful."

"See here..."

Lincoln waved his drink. "How are we going to check up on you?"

"Surely my word is good enough."

Cubby rubbed his hands together like a theatrical villain. "I shall keep a watchful eye on Mr. Chippington-Smythe. Be so good as to inform me of the location of your lodgings when you find them."

"Won't you be a little obvious?"

"I shall be in disguise, Sir."

"You could pass for a cyclops without too much makeup," I muttered. "See here, if Cubby's bumbling gives me away then I win. It's only fair."

"Fine."

Cubby gave Ford a conspiratorial wink. "Never fear, Sir. I believe your bar tab is as good as paid."

Binky grabbed my arm. "We've got to start training. Let's get you to Bentley before we lose another second."

We raced out of the bar on tottering heels and headed for home to begin my training.

CHAPTER TWO

An Education

Whenever thinking rears its ugly head I turn to Bentley, my miraculous mechanical manservant. He has been my constant companion since birth and served the same function for my father and his father before him. I have found that making a move without him invariably leads to catastrophe. He listened with his head cocked slightly to one side.

"So that's the ghastly situation in a nutshell, Bentley. What are your thoughts?"

There was a surprisingly long pause, during which I could hear Bentley's gears grinding away like a flour mill. Finally, he chugged back into animation and regarded me gravely.

"I am afraid, Sir, that I deeply disapprove of this venture. I warn you against it most seriously. My advice is to declare the bet lost and to pay the required bar tabs."

I regarded him with astonishment. "Wave the white flag? Really?"

Binky's eyes were rolling about in their sockets. "Look here, that's all well and good for Cyril, who's rich as Midas, but I'm on the hook too and I can barely pay my *own* bar bill."

"I am afraid that I have no advice on that subject, Sir."

This defeatist attitude was unlike Bentley's usual sanguine outlook.

"But why are you so set against it? Do you fear for my safety?"

"No, Sir. Thanks to constant surveillance, DNA data banks and a vigorous network of informants, there has not been a crime among the economically disadvantaged for decades."

"Then what?"

"It is unseemly, Sir. It is not the thing."

"Explain yourself."

"Poverty, Sir, is not a fit subject for frivolity. It is a state contrary to the dignity that is owed to each member of the human race. It is a plague and a disgrace and to pretend to be a victim of it for spurious reasons dishonours you."

"But we're not talking about poverty. We're talking about ordinary people. The people you see protesting on the street every day."

"Those are the poor, Sir."

"But they receive free food and shelter. And free hydrogen, let's not forget—from my plants. Damned generous of me I must say."

"The government pays you for the hydrogen, Sir. The business is quite profitable."

"Is it? I suppose you would know."

Binky huffed and puffed. "Stop trying to sabotage him. This is a matter of honour."

"Yes, he's right, Bentley. A bet is a challenge. I must meet it or be shamed."

Bentley focused his optic sensors on me for a long moment. "If that is your understanding of shame then perhaps this enterprise will be an education for you. I withdraw my objections. I believe that you should go."

Binky clapped his hands with delight. "That's more like it."

"What should I do first?"

"I shall procure clothing more appropriate for you, and I believe that we should acquire a tutor, Sir."

"A tutor?"

"Someone who lives the life of an ordinary citizen and can guide you through the minutiae of their daily lives. I have someone in mind."

"Who?"

"The young man who delivers your groceries may serve our purpose. He is due at any moment."

"Excellent. Binky and I will practice walking and talking like ordinary people while you get on with your preparations."

Bentley raised a metallic eyebrow. "It's a pity that your efforts cannot be recorded for posterity, Sir."

"Thank you, Bentley. Very flattering. Off you go. We've got work to do."

He whooshed away and we set about my transformation. Binky regarded me judiciously.

"You should kick off those heels."

I did so and scrunched my toes into the carpet. "Ah. That's more like it."

"Now walk up and down."

I strolled back and forth a few times.

"You're rolling your hips too much."

"That's the way I walk."

"Well, it looks like you're enjoying yourself. The poor walk to get somewhere."

"How would you know how or why the poor walk?"

"You forget my theatrical training at University."

I didn't forget—I had mercifully blacked it out.

"We were taught how to observe humanity. It's called symphony... or empathy... or timpani. I do it all the time."

"I thought you were just staring into space."

"It is sometimes difficult to tell the difference, even for me. Now try again."

I strode up and down.

"Better. Try it without the humming."

"What's wrong with humming?"

"You still seem like you're enjoying yourself too much. Try frowning."

I scowled. "Like this?"

"That's not a frown. You're crossing your eyes."

"Show me what you mean."

He contorted his face into something vaguely reminiscent of the Kabuki Theater. "Like this."

"Is it necessary to pucker your lips like a fish?"

"I wasn't."

"You certainly were."

He shook his face back and forth and blew air loudly through his lips. "Let's come back to that. Try talking like an ordinary person."

"What does that mean?"

"Without any ornamentation. Short. To the point. 'Hey, you. What are you doing? Hey, it looks like rain.' That sort of thing."

"Hey. Where are you going, Old Man?"

"Lose the 'Old Man.'"

"Hey. Where you going?"

"Better."

"Where can a fellow get a drink around here?" I paused thoughtfully. "Should I spit?"

"Can you?"

"I think so."

"Not on the carpet. Bentley would disapprove."

"What if I were to scratch myself?"

Binky looked doubtful. "Where?"

"The nether regions?"

"Steady! Let's walk before we try to fly."

Just then Bentley entered, followed by a rather tousled young man in a white delivery coat. "This is Ernie, Sir."

"Just Ernie?"

The young man tipped his cap. "Yes, Sir."

"No last name?"

"Can't afford one, Sir."

Bentley cleared his throat. "I have explained the situation to Ernie. He has agreed to tutor you on the subject of how to pass as a member of the general population."

"Damned decent of you, Ernie."

"Happy to help, Sir."

"Perhaps you shouldn't call me 'Sir.' I'll have to get used to doing without that."

Ernie scratched his chin uncomfortably. "All right... you."

"Allow me to introduce Mr. Wickford-Davies."

"Pleased to meet you S... guy."

Binky shoved out a paw. You can still call me 'Sir,' if it's easier."

"Thank you, Sir. It ties your brain up in knots—going against your conditioning like this."

I rubbed my hands eagerly. "So, Ernie, what should we do first?"

"Well... I guess we should figure out some things... like where are you going to stay?"

"At a hotel, I suppose."

"We don't have hotels."

"Where do travelers reside?"

"Travel is too expensive for most of us. If you have to go somewhere you just stay with family, or a friend."

"I have neither."

"Why don't you stay with my family?"

"Would they mind?"

"No. People stay with us all the time. It's small, but we're pretty comfortable. I'll tell them you're an old school friend."

Binky perked up. "You went to school?"

"Until I had to get a job."

"So, you can read?"

"I read whenever I've got a free moment."

Binky looked wistful. "Reading irritates my eyes."

"Maybe you need glasses."

Binky stiffened. "Gentlemen do not wear glasses. It smacks of trying."

"Bentley reads things out loud to me. Damned convenient."

Ernie stared at me. "But you can read if you have to?"

"I think so. Will it be necessary on this venture?"

"I suppose you could get by without it, but it's handy for things like street signs."

"This is all so interesting. It's as if there's a whole world one knew nothing about."

Ernie looked at me oddly. "Yes. It's called... the world."

Bentley slid in with an armful of material. "I took the liberty of acquiring some garments, Sir."

Ernie picked at the pile doubtfully. "That's government-issue stuff. Watch out for pins—there's usually a few left in the seams."

"Step behind this screen, Sir, and we'll try them on for size."

In what seemed like mere moments I stood in a loose-fitting shirt and trousers.

"Are these the undergarments? Where is the rest of it?"

"This completes the ensemble, Sir."

"What? No girdle?"

"No, Sir."

"It leaves my midsection rather flapping in the breeze, what?"

"I believe you will become accustomed to it"

I strolled out from behind the screen and made a few passes up and down the room. "Well?"

Binky looked scandalized. "It's almost indecent."

"It's what everyone wears," observed Ernie.

"I must say it's damned comfortable."

Bentley handed me a flimsy pair of sandals. "Your flip-flops, Sir."

I dangled them on a finger. "Insubstantial."

Binky peered at them. "How do they stay on?"

I experimented a bit. "It seems one grips them between the big and second toe."

"Don't try to run in them. You'll fall," Ernie warned.

"Is that why the masses always seem to walk in such a lackadaisical fashion?"

"No, they're just exhausted."

"From what?"

"From living. Most people have more than one job."

"But what do you need money for? You pay no rent. Your food is provided for you. Even my hydrogen is subsidized."

Ernie squinted at me. "When you say 'food,' do you mean nutrition bars?"

"I don't know. Is that what they give you?"

"That is *all* they give us. They keep you alive—barely. And the taste! I don't know if you've ever licked the mold that grows in the corner of your refrigerator but that should give you a rough idea."

Binky sniffed. "I suppose you have a bone to pick with his free hydrogen as well?"

"Well... I didn't like to say, but there is some resentment among the general population."

I was startled. "Why? What's wrong with my hydrogen?"

"Nothing—in principle, but the system is rife with corruption. The government pays for it and that means politicians have access to all that money, so it gets siphoned off at every level. By the time it reaches us the hydrogen travels through leaky, rusting pipes that often burst into flames. Even at the best of times we only get gas for a few hours a day."

"Monstrous! They should protest."

"They do protest. You can hear them from your window."

"Why isn't something done?"

"You can't expect politicians to do the right thing. The person that could do something is the owner of the hydrogen plants."

"Well, he ought to be held accountable."

Bentley made a little "hem" sound. "I'm afraid he is speaking of you, Sir."

"Me? What have I to do with it?"

"You are the owner of the plants, Sir."

"But I don't actually have anything to do with them, you know."

Ernie shook his head. "The people don't know that. I'm afraid they blame you."

"What, by name?"

"Oh yes. Your name is prominently featured in the protest chants."

"Cyril Chippington-Smythe?"

"Yes. The rhymes are pretty bad. "Chippington-Smythe is not very nythe". That sort of thing. It works when a thousand people are chanting it."

"Bentley! Were you aware of this?"

"I saw no point in bringing it to your attention until something could be done, Sir."

"And what is to be done?"

"I am still formulating a plan."

A sudden thought froze my blood. "But if they discover me among them, they'll tear me to pieces!"

Ernie nodded. "You should use a false name."

Binky practically leapt into the air. "Oh, let me think of one! I love false names!" He strode about, rubbing his nose and emitting a string of "ums" and "ers." Finally, he whirled around and pointed at me.

"Eustace Chippington-Smythe!"

Ernie looked doubtful. "I think the Chippington-Smythe part is still a giveaway, Sir."

He "um'd" and "er'd" some more. "Cyril Wallingford-Jones!"

Ernie thought for a moment. "What about Johny?"

"Just Johny?"

"Most people don't use a last name. It's considered putting on airs."

I tried it out. "Johny. Hey, Johny! Good on you, Johny. Johny, could you come here for a moment? I rather like it."

Binky stuck out his lower lip. "I still think mine were better."

"Don't sulk. This is my new life. I am Johny: a devil-may-care jack-of-all-trades with a nasty temper and a wicked left hook."

Binky turned to Ernie. "What do you think? Will he pass?"

Ernie looked me up and down. "I wish his teeth weren't so good, but he'll do. Shall I pick you up tomorrow morning and walk you over to my family's flat?"

"Yes. One more night of luxury on the old silk sheets and I'll be ready for adventure. Bentley, send Ernie's address to Cubby Martinez at the club. We must be vigilant. He'll be watching me like a hawk."

"What would you like for your last meal, Sir? Tacos?"

"Of course! I said luxury and I meant it. Binky, Ernie, would you care to stay for some tacos?"

Ernie shook his head. "I'm afraid I have to get to my next job."

Binky was salivating. "Well, I'm in. I haven't been able to wallow in tacos since I won that sweepstakes last May. Plenty of salsa, Bentley."

"Of course, Sir."

As I continued to stride back and forth, feeling a distinct breeze on unaccustomed parts of my anatomy, I reflected that clothes did, indeed, make the man, and that the person I saw leering back at me from my looking glass was someone I would cross the street to avoid. This was a creature that scoffed at hardships, sneered at impediments and chortled at danger. "Bentley!"

"Sir?"

"No cutlery. I'll eat the tacos with my hands."

"As you wish, Sir. Very virile of you, I'm sure."

"You know... I'm looking forward to this. It's going to be fun!"

And, ignoring the chill that ran down my spine, I took another whack at frowning and stalked like a panther toward the tacos that cowered on the dining room table.

CHAPTER THREE

A Harrowing Journey

Ernie arrived, as promised, with the morning lark. He waited patiently as I downed a breakfast that would have choked the mythical horse. Bentley had helped me into my government-issued rags and my pockets were filled with coins of low denomination and crackers of various descriptions. I had slathered on the deodorant, having learned that fresh water was in short supply among the general population, and I was ready for anything.

"Very well, Ernie. Off we go."

"It's a bit of a trek, I'm afraid."

"Should I have Bentley drive us partway?"

"Too dangerous, Sir. Gossip travels like lightning. If anyone saw you..."

"I quite understand. Let's be off!"

Ernie did not exaggerate. We walked for what felt like hours. The posts of my flip-flops rubbed against my toes until I wanted to scream.

"Surely we must be there!"

Ernie looked at me curiously. "We've only traveled a few blocks. You can still see your house from here."

"How many miles is that?"

"None."

"This is torture!"

It seemed my adventure was over before it had begun. I began to estimate the next year's bar tab in my head.

Ernie was concentrating fiercely. "I have an idea. Wait here."

He jogged off and I took stock of my surroundings. Even in the few blocks we had traversed the buildings had grown shabbier—the weeds more numerous. As I stood musing, I heard the clatter of an approaching vehicle. It appeared to be a stagecoach of the Old West variety, drawn by six mechanical horses. A grizzled automaton sat atop it gripping the reins. As it reached me the coach slowed to a stop and a familiar pomaded head popped out of the window. C. Langford-Cheeseworth was as rich as he was eccentric. He was the club gossip and I knew that my ragged appearance would be common knowledge by lunchtime. I suspected that the general assessment upon learning of my situation would be that I had made a bigger ass of myself than usual.

"Cywil! Death before dishonour. What scrofulous apparel! Are you *en woute* to a costume party?"

"Hallo, Cheeseworth. Death before dishonour. Yes, something like that."

"I simply wevel in costume balls. May I accompany you? I always keep a spare disguise with me. There's an anatomically cowwect dolphin in the boot. One welieves oneself thwough the blowhole."

"Sorry Cheeseworth. It's not exactly a costume party. Er... it's something new. It's called... slumming."

"I am agog! What are the mechanics of this new form of entertainment?"

"Well... one dresses as a citizen and... lives like a citizen... among the citizens you see."

He cackled. "Like Marie Antoinette when she dwessed as a shepherdess and swanned about her little make-believe hamlet at Versailles!"

"Yes. Something like that."

"Wemarkable! Who else is going?"

"Oh... everyone's doing it!"

His face fell. "Are they? Why wasn't I told?"

"It's brand new. I'm sure you'll hear all about it any minute."

"Well, *bonne chance*! I want a full weport of your adventures when you weturn."

"Absolutely! We'll make a night of it."

The automaton flipped his whip and the horses galloped off with Cheeseworth rattling along behind them. Just then Ernie rounded the corner pushing an unsightly wheeled object.

"Here we are. Hop on."

"What is this?"

"It's my delivery cart. I'll push you."

I examined it doubtfully. "Are you sure it will take the weight?"

"You're really rather scrawny, if you don't mind my saying."

I drew myself up to my full height. "You're seeing me without my padding. I assure you I am a damned attractive figure of a man, given a *soupçon* of mechanical assistance."

"No doubt. Just hold on to the sides and I'll have you there in an instant."

I perched on the delivery cart like a sack of root vegetables and clung to the slats for dear life. Ernie trotted up hill and down dale, through blocks of abandoned structures and weed-filled lots. He leaned over the handle toward me.

"If we meet anyone, we'll say you twisted your ankle."

"Shall I groan and wince?"

"Not necessary." He considered. "Maybe a slight wince the first time you put weight on it."

I practiced wincing for a while, then sat back and watched the scenery go by as I munched on crackers from my various pockets.

"I say, Ernie?"

"Yep?"

"I notice a lot of abandoned buildings. Why is your family crammed into a tiny flat with all of this real estate available?"

"It's private property. No one can live there."

"But what do the owners do with the empty buildings?"

"They tear them down and plant soybeans."

"Soybeans? Is that profitable?"

"Thanks to government subsidies. They collect subsidies to grow soybeans, then the government pays them to store the soybeans, then pays them again to compost the soy beans to fertilize their soybean fields."

"But who eats the soybeans?"

"A small fraction of them are turned into the kind of imitation food that rich people eat, but the rest get composted."

"Then what are nutrition bars made of?"

"Heaven knows. There's no list of ingredients. They seem to be mostly algae. We suspect there are barbiturates in them to keep us placid and birth control to keep the population down. We only eat them when we absolutely have to."

"Monstrous!"

He eyed me carefully. "Do you know that you manufacture them?"

"I don't think so."

"Fruity Berry Blast bars are made by Smythe Corporation. That's you."

"I don't pay attention to what my businesses do. That's what my financial managers are for."

"Perhaps you should take an interest."

"I don't know. My past forays into business have not augured well."

"We're getting closer. I think you should climb down and hobble the last couple of blocks."

I eased myself off of the cart and brushed the cracker crumbs from my lap.

"What a grueling journey. So, this is where you live?"

Chez Ernie was in an area that might have been called "blighted" if one wanted to be complimentary. The pavement had petered out several blocks earlier and a trail of dust and rocks ran between a canyon of decaying buildings. The local populace, attired in the same class of rags as I, trudged here and there lugging this and that and looking miserable. Ernie pointed at the most disreputable of the structures.

"That's home. If we get separated meet me in the lobby."

"Got it."

"Before we go up, let's talk to my sister Judy about finding you a job."

I recoiled. "Is that strictly necessary?"

"Everyone works. It would be suspicious if you just sat around doing nothing."

"But I have no qualifications. I'm not skilled in any way."

"That's no impediment. Anything that requires any skill is done by robots anyway."

"Then what's left?"

He considered. "Well, there's carrying things. That's what a lot of people do. You pick up something at one location and carry it somewhere else. It requires a certain amount of muscle, so maybe that's not for you."

"I am susceptible to sprains."

"Then there's gas leak locating. They give you a roll of tape and you stroll about sniffing at gas pipes. If you smell a leak, you wrap some tape around it."

"It sounds dangerous."

"Only if you have an open flame about you."

"Anything else?"

"My sister is a waiter."

"Oh, in a restaurant?"

"No. That's another job for robots. She waits in lines."

I ran this around the old squirrel cage. "She just... waits?"

"Yes. There's lots of important things one has to line up for but you can't take time off from work to do it, so people like Judy wait in line for you. It doesn't pay much but it's steady."

"That sounds as if it is within my abilities. Years of standing at soirees have given me the endurance of Atlas."

"Good. I think she's at the insurance adjuster's office today. Now remember, your name is Johny."

"Got it."

Before we set off, I paused at the entrance to Ernie's building and looked around carefully. Across the street in one of the windows I spotted what could have been a reflection from a pair of binoculars. Cubby! I turned nonchalantly and strolled off down the street.

Ernie looked at me earnestly. "Now listen, Judy's a good egg but she's nobody's fool. You'll have to look sharp. No slip-ups."

"I am completely in character. Watch this."

I had practiced spitting that morning in the garden with Bentley and felt that I had grasped the rudiments. I went through the steps in order, but what should have been a projectile wound up decorating the front of my shirt.

"Well, I'll have to work on my distance, but I thought the attitude was spot on."

"Here, wipe yourself with these leaves. There she is. Oy! Judy!"

A vivacious young lady waved to us from a long line of bored-looking citizens. "Ernie! Why aren't you at work?"

"I finished my deliveries early. This is Johny."

"Hallo," I chirped winningly.

She scanned me up and down. "Hiya Johny. You're not from around here."

"How could you tell?"

"You've got all your fingernails."

I shoved out a mitt. "I'm deuced glad to meet you."

"That's a funny way of talking."

Ernie didn't miss a beat. "Yes! He's... from Wales."

"Is that how they talk in Wales?"

I wriggled uncomfortably. "When we speak at all. We Welsh are a taciturn race."

"He came here to get a waiting job."

"Don't they have waiters in Wales?"

I tried to look sad. "It's the nepotism! Waiting jobs passed from one generation to the next. Couldn't get a foothold. Greener pastures and all that."

She shrugged. "Suit yourself."

"Do you think you could get him started, Sis?"

"Sure. I'll talk to my supervisor after work." She turned to me. "How's your bladder?"

I stared. "My what?"

"No bathroom breaks. You step out of line you lose your place."

"Ah. As to that, I am known for the infrequency of my urinations."

"You talk pretty fancy for a waiter."

Ernie gave me a warning glance. "He reads a lot."

"Does he? What are you reading now?"

When it comes to titles of books, I'm afraid the last one that stuck was *Two Bunnies Step Out* and that didn't seem likely to impress. Ernie saw my hesitation and jumped in.

"You're working your way through *War and Peace*, aren't you Johny?"

"Yes! I'm still slogging through the war bits, but you can just get a hint of approaching peace in the syntax."

Judy seemed impressed. "I guess you *are* a reader."

"I'm going to drag him back to meet Mum. Are you coming home for dinner?"

"I think so. The line's moving a little faster since some of the older waiters fainted from the heat."

"See you there, then."

"Pleased to meet you Johny. I'll let you know what my supervisor says."

"Thanks awfully."

Ernie and I picked our way back through the broken streets to his apartment building.

"It's five flights to the apartment. Can you make it?"

I stared at him, appalled. "Five flights of stairs?"

"Yes. I don't think I can carry you. We can stop whenever you need to rest."

I did rather well, if I do say so, stopping every half-flight to sit and munch a few crackers. By late-afternoon we were standing outside an apartment door that had been lovingly painted a vibrant shade of blue.

"This is it."

I straightened myself up, patted myself down, brushed myself off, and prepared myself for whatever lay ahead.

Chapter Four

I Eat a Cherry

Ernie opened the door and we stepped into a tiny jewel box of an apartment. Every surface had been painted with swirls and loops of color. Bits of shiny metal and glass were embedded here and there.

"My word. This is lovely."

"That's all Judy's work. She's artistic. Hello, Mum."

A middle-aged matron with a gray bun on top of her head was standing over a sink doing something to a pile of greenery. "Hello, love. Who's this?"

"This is Johny. He's an old school chum. He's come to stay for the week."

"How do, Johny! Excuse me not shaking hands. I'm up to my elbows in dandelion greens."

"Pleased to meet you."

"Will you be joining us for supper?"

"Thanks awfully. I'd love to, if it's not too much bother."

"Course. Share and share alike. All is for all. To each according to his need."

Ernie winked at me. "Mum's a socialist."

"And what are you?"

"Not in front of a guest, Mum."

"Does he not feel the lash of poverty? Come the revolution no doubt he'll march like the rest of us."

"I would be honoured. When is it?"

"It'll be here before you know it... and the streets will run with blood. Wipe your feet."

"Sorry, Mum."

She turned back to her greens. "Don't pay any attention to me, Johny. I've got a bark that's worse than my bite."

"You should meet my Aunt Hypatia. You two have a lot in common."

Ernie tugged on my elbow. "Come on, let me show you around."

Though it was tiny, the apartment was dense. Ingenious cupboards and drawers were everywhere. Ernie led me to a section of wall that was painted a deep blue.

"This is my little corner. The bed folds down from the wall."

Every surface was covered with drawings of machines of one kind or another interspersed with what I had been told in my youth were numbers.

"What's all this?"

Ernie looked sheepish. "Oh... I like to invent things in my spare time. It's just a hobby."

I inspected them more closely. "Damned fine drawings. What's this one?"

He lit up with enthusiasm. "That's something I call a bulb of light."

"What's it do?"

"It replaces gaslights."

"How does it work?"

"It doesn't... yet. You see, most of my inventions are based on a force that doesn't exist, except in nature. You can see it in lightning storms. Lightning contains incredible power. I was outside during a storm once and a bolt of lightning hit close by. I felt as if I was in a glass of fizzy water. The hairs on my head stood straight up. A tree nearby exploded from the power of it. I realized that there is a natural force that, if it could be harnessed, could usher in a new age of technology. I call it, 'fizzy energy.'"

"My word! That is exciting!"

"I just have to find a way to control it, or produce it."

"And it would light up your bulb of light?"

"Not just that. It could power motors with more power and less expense than steam, and it would be loads safer than hydrogen."

"Well, I certainly wish you luck."

"Thanks. I'm closing in on the theory. That's what all these equations are."

"It seems you're wasted delivering groceries."

"Oh, I could never give up my delivery job. There aren't many professions available to us with the kind of future you get in the delivery game."

As I gazed around the room I was suddenly struck with a terrifying apprehension. "I say, Ernie?"

"Yep?"

"You all sleep here? In one room?"

"That's pretty common."

"But then... where do I sleep?"

"You'll bunk with me. You get half a mattress all to yourself."

Now I like to think of myself as resilient. I have a guest room and once or twice there have even been guests in it. I have never complained. Sharing a bedroom, however, much less a mattress, was beyond the pale. I halted toward the apartment door on shaking legs. A dark spot appeared in the center of my vision.

"Where are you going?"

"I wave the white flag. All is lost."

"Don't give up. It's not as bad as it seems."

"Why is there no air in here? My lungs don't seem to be functioning."

As I approached the door it flew open from the other side and Judy breezed in. "Hallo, all! Johny, congratulations. You start in the morning. Be at the tax office at seven A.M. Say, are you all right?"

Ernie shoved a chair behind my knees, which felt increasingly watery. I collapsed back onto it.

"He's just having a little panic attack."

Judy eyed me with concern. "What brought this on?"

"Er... homesickness. Misses Wales. Wants to go home."

"Aw, you poor fish. Say, maybe you're just hungry. Here, Mum, hand me that bowl of cherries."

Their mum handed over a large bowl filled with bright red spheres. Judy picked out a particularly rosy specimen. "Here you go."

She waited until my mouth opened to exhale and shoved the sphere into it. I bit down and an elixir filled my mouth that absolutely paralyzed me.

"What!? What in the name of all that is holy... is that?!"

"It's a cherry, silly."

My heart was racing. "A... cherry?"

Judy laughed merrily. "They grow on trees. Don't you have them in Wales?"

Ernie grabbed a handful of the fruit under discussion. "Of course they do. He's just having a laugh."

Their mother took the bowl. "That's enough. You two set up the table. Food's ready."

"Sure thing, Mum."

I watched the bowl depart wistfully. "Will there be more... cherries?"

"That's dessert. First, we'll have a bit of salad, then pasta with marinara and fresh baked bread."

Judy put a cool hand on my forehead. "Are you feeling better?"

"Yes... I am. I really am. I think... I could eat something."

"Just stay there. We'll set up the table around you."

They produced a folding table and chairs and everything was set up in a trice. Judy put a large bowl filled with greens before us. Mum took off her apron and sat.

"Here's dandelion greens, lamb's quarters and wild onions in a vinaigrette. Dig in, everyone."

What followed was the greatest meal of my life. Leaves! Leaves that grew in the ground! Who suspected they could be eaten in this unprocessed form? And the tomato sauce! Not at all like the dipping sauce that came with my pizza rolls. Complex, with sweetness and acidity in just the right proportions. I ate until I could hold no more. Judy regarded me with amusement.

"I'd say Johny likes Mum's cooking all right."

Mum smiled. "He's a man who knows what's good."

I shifted in my seat to allow my midsection more freedom. "Do you eat like this every night?"

"On a weekday we don't try too hard. Turnip casserole, Vichyssoise. We get a little more creative on the weekends."

I leaned over to murmur in Ernie's ear. "Look here, Ernie, I've got to speak to you. Is there somewhere we can go?"

"Let's take a stroll."

I eyed him with alarm. "What, down the stairs?"

"Sure."

"And then back up the stairs?"

Judy caught the last bit of our interchange. "Don't they have stairs in Wales?"

I had gotten into character by now and the improvisations were flowing out of me. "Mostly low-rises. On account of the earthquakes."

"I never heard of earthquakes in Wales."

"We hush it up. Silly Welsh pride. Come, Ernie, let's take a walk."

I waited until we had reached the street and found a quiet patch of dirt where we wouldn't be overheard. I whirled around to face him. "All right, my lad, what the blazes was that?"

He looked at me with bewilderment. "What?"

"That meal? Where did that come from?"

"That's the way we always eat."

"Then why have I been swilling down impossible mutton and pizza rolls since childhood? Why have I been deprived of this ambrosia?"

"Because there's no profit in the kind of food we eat. It just grows in the ground. The money's in the processing."

"And I could have been eating like this my whole life?"

"Sure."

At that moment I was filled with a cold fury—a hatred of those who had stuffed me with improbable bacon and chickeny nuggets for their own selfish profits. "Who are these monsters? These profiteers that hold our taste buds for ransom?"

"I'm afraid it's SmytheCo again."

"What? I've been doing it to myself?"

"'Fraid so."

A wind seemed to blow through my very soul. "Ernie, I am a changed man. I have found my purpose in life. It is to eat like this every day until I die."

"Well, it's good to have a goal."

"Where do these fruits and vegetables come from?"

"Everybody's got a garden or two. Vacant lots, odd bits of land that haven't got soybeans on them. Pots on the roof. Vegetables grow anywhere there's dirt."

"And it's all free?"

"There are some things we can't grow ourselves—flour, oil, salt. We trade for those if we can. There's volunteer collectives that have built mills and oil presses. It's a kind of underground."

"Amazing. In some ways you live better than I do."

"Money isn't everything."

"I said that just the other day at the club."

"See? You're practically one of us already. If you had fewer teeth and a little sun damage, you'd fit right in. Ready for some cherries?"

"You bet I am. Bring on those stairs."

As we trudged back toward Ernie's flat, I suddenly felt dizzy. "I say, Ernie?"

"Yes Johny?"

"I'm afraid I'm not well. I'm beginning to hallucinate."

"What do you think you see?"

"I have the oddest feeling that those citizens in rags waving at us from the corner are my aunt and uncle and that the shiny-headed pauper rooting through that garbage can is C. Langford-Cheeseworth."

"Yoo-hoo! Johny!"

Alas, it was no hallucination. My Aunt Hypatia, dressed as a theatrical version of a charwoman, was waving at me like a character from a Punch and Judy show. My Uncle Hugo stood glowering beside her in a sort of sack that must have held potatoes at some point in its existence... and from the shadow of a doorway, his head bowed with shame, stepped the Judas that I knew at once must be responsible for this catastrophe—my chinless cousin, Binky.

"Hallo, Cyril... I mean Johny! I can explain all this."

My spirit, which had been buoyed up by dinner, poured itself a large vodka and began reading Russian literature. If this was not the end of my story it was certainly the end of a chapter.

CHAPTER FIVE

A Detour

It is generally believed that family is a nourishing force in one's life. It was also believed for centuries that the Sun rotated around the Earth. In my experience aunts and uncles exist to shed light on one's deficiencies, and cousins are a plague akin to scabies. There was certainly no way I could win my bet with this circus side show orbiting around me and the beady-eyed Cubby Martinez camped across the road peering through his binoculars.

"Look here, Ernie, perhaps I should speak to them alone."

"All right. I'll meet you back at the apartment."

"Thanks awfully. I won't be long. Save me some cherries."

Ernie ambled off and I took a deep breath. "Aunt! Uncle! Cheeseworth! Binky! Death before dishonour. What on earth are you doing here?"

Binky threw up his hands. "It's not my fault!"

My aunt adjusted her charwoman costume. She had somehow contrived to make her collection of dust rags look fashionable. "Death before dishonour, darling boy."

"Death before dishonour," growled Uncle Hugo.

"Death before dishonour, Cywil! We're slumming! I've never had such wiotous fun!"

"Slumming, are you? Well, I hope you've enjoyed your little day trip. No doubt you can't wait to get back to civilization."

My aunt gazed at me benevolently. "But darling, we've come for the week, like you."

Without his customary monocle and walking stick, Cheeseworth didn't know what to do with his hands. They fluttered nervously around him like birds. "Binky told us everything. You're going by the alias 'Johny' and living the carefwee life of the peasantwy."

I glanced around nervously. "For heaven's sake, don't call them 'the peasantry' unless you want to be chased with torches."

Cheeseworth frowned. "You're wight. I must stifle my natural condescension."

I gaped at them all hopelessly. "But where are you all staying? There are no hotels."

Cheeseworth brightened. "It's too divine! I had my land yacht disguised as a cargo twuck. Come and see!"

They led me around the corner and there, parked in a weed-choked lot, was a rust-covered vehicle roughly the size of a freight car.

"It's twompe l'oeil! I had a team of artists working on it all day."

As we drew closer, I could see that the rust was carefully painted on, along with dead leaves and faded graffiti. Cheeseworth led us to the side of the vehicle and pressed a nearly invisible button. A concealed door swung open and a spring-loaded set of stairs unfolded.

"*Entrez, s'il vous plait.*"

My aunt clapped her hands. "Hugo, we must acquire one of these vehicles."

"Over my dead body."

She bestowed a withering glare on him. "A prophecy that may prove all too accurate."

As I climbed the steps, the inside of the truck filled with light from gas fed chandeliers and I beheld a wonder to rival Ali Baba's treasure cave. Every surface was gilded or upholstered in luxurious fabric. A table was set in the center of the room and next to it stood Mrs. Cedar, the Cheeseworth family's mechanical housekeeper, holding a platter of hors d'oeuvres.

"What are these wefweshments, Mrs. Cedar?"

"Pate of sea creatures, Sir."

My aunt waved the platter away. "I am deathly allergic to shellfish."

"Not to worry, Ma'am. There are no actual sea creatures in it."

"That is a relief. Apparently, the name is meant to be poetic rather than descriptive."

Cheeseworth threw off his ragged coat and retrieved a jeweled monocle from a tray on the sideboard. "Make yourselves at home, everyone."

My aunt lowered herself into an armchair and munched a cracker. "I suppose you're wondering how we all came to be here?"

"It had crossed my mind."

Cheeseworth cackled. "It's all my fault, dear boy. After you told me about slumming I couldn't west until I had twied it. I wan into Binky at the club and was surpwised at how weticent he was to weveal the details of your excursion but in the end, I winkled it out of him. He insisted on coming along. I knew Hypatia would love it."

My aunt sniffed. "And Hugo came as a necessary appendage."

"Thank you very much."

Binky was eyeing me nervously and picking at his burlap. "I told them how frightfully important it is not to reveal your true nature to the local populace, and to call you Johny at all times."

My aunt nodded. "We quite understand. The adulation of the masses is a terrible burden. I myself experienced it when I chaired a charity bazaar. Apparently, I possess an overabundance of charisma. I had not a moment's peace. I would not repeat the experience for any amount of money."

"What was the charity?"

"Oh, I don't remember. We were selling orphans or some such nonsense."

My uncle sputtered. "Finding homes for orphans, not selling them."

"It amounts to the same thing, doesn't it?"

I stood and paced. "Look here, it's crucial that everyone here believes that I am not special in any way."

"That requires no subterfuge—it is simply the truth."

"Yes! Thank you, Uncle Hugo."

My aunt patted my hand indulgently. "It's too delicious! But my dear, you must sleep here with us. There are the most perfect little bedrooms in the back. You'll have one all to yourself."

I have never believed that temptation is a thing to be resisted. On the one hand was a charming little compartment in Cheeseworth's rolling palace with a luxurious bed in it and on the other—half a mattress in a crowded studio. Why did I hesitate? Was it the thought that Ernie and his family would be... disappointed? Or was it curiosity at what wonders might appear on their breakfast table? No one was more surprised than I to hear me saying, "Thanks awfully, but I've got a place to stay."

"With a local?"

"Yes. A lovely family. They've invited me in."

My aunt shook her head. "You really are taking this slumming to an almost obscene level of authenticity."

"If a thing's worth doing it's worth doing well. That's a saying, isn't it?"

"Suit yourself, Nephew. Now tell us of your adventures."

"Well! This has been an eye-opener and no mistake. Our ideas about how the huddled masses live couldn't be more mistaken."

Aunt Hypatia raised a hand. "Produce an example. I cannot abide generalities. They make me feel as if others know more than me, which is insupportable."

"For starters, they eat better than we do."

"Impossible. My grocery bill would bankrupt a pasha."

"It turns out that you can grow your own food for free and it's delicious."

"The fact that it is free is all you need to know. If a thing costs nothing it follows that it is worth nothing. That is known as philosophy."

My uncle chimed in. "The high prices that we pay for our food ensure that it is beyond the reach of all but the wealthy. Exclusivity ensures quality. It is one of the perks of being rich."

I looked around at them. "But it tastes awful, doesn't it? Is it just me?"

Cheeseworth shook his head sadly. "Poor Cywil. Being among these people even for a day has given you a condition known as "Stockholm Syndwome". It was named for a scientist who visited Sweden for a month and found that he developed a craving for lutefisk, which is generally known to be vile. Your taste buds have been bwainwashed."

"No, you must try it. You'll see."

"I have no intention of succumbing to dysentery," huffed my aunt. "We have brought packaged food and water for the week. That is sufficient."

Binky stared at me enviously. "Have you really eaten the local food? How brave you are. Do you think I would like it?"

"My boy, you'd love it. If you can buck the tide of public opinion, I'll take you to a meal you will never forget."

"I say, I'm in."

My aunt shook her head disapprovingly. "Just don't bring anything communicable back to the land yacht."

"What else have you discovered on your peregrinations?" asked Cheeseworth.

"Well, there's a terrible scandal going on with soybeans."

My uncle rose to his feet. "I must stop you there. The planting and composting of soybeans is one of Smythe Corporation's largest profit centers."

"Well, I'm not going to stand for it anymore."

"You comprehend that your aunt's fortune is largely based on her holdings of stock in your company?"

Cheeseworth toyed with his monocle nervously. "Mine as well. Everything I have is tied up in Smythe Corporation Stock. If you upend the business, I'll be wuined!"

"I'm afraid that ends the discussion," declared my aunt. "Family comes first. You must protect the profits of Smythe Corporation above all other considerations."

"But... we're doing terrible things."

"That is all dependent upon your perspective," observed Uncle Hugo.

My aunt raised a powdered hand. "It is said that behind every great fortune is a great crime. It follows that a fortune as immense as ours must require an ongoing series of great crimes to sustain itself. That is science, and therefore indisputable."

"Look here, I can't very well go on as if nothing was wrong. We're poisoning people! Forcing them into substandard living conditions! Taking away any hope of fulfilling employment!"

Uncle Hugo peered at his steepled fingers judiciously. "Those with the qualities necessary to rise above their condition will thrive. The rest are clearly satisfied to stay as they are."

"That's... I mean to say... dash it all..."

My aunt's eyes narrowed. "Either compose a sentence or stare into space. This sputtering is most unattractive."

"You're being deucedly unsympathetic."

"There must be poor people in order for there to be wich people. It is the contwast which defines us."

"Yes," my aunt agreed. "It is our differences which give savour to life. If we were all equal life would be like a tepid bath."

"I cannot subscribe to this point of view. These people are my friends."

My aunt looked grim. "And we are family, which is the opposite of friendship. You must make a choice."

"Then I choose friendship."

"Beware. Friendship is a bubble, blown hither and yon by every fickle breeze. Family is like a suit of lead—stable, substantial, inescapable."

"Keep your leaden vestments. You may cower here in your gilded cage. I will cast my lot with the people. Good day!"

I started for the door.

"But Cywil..."

"I said good day!"

Binky gave a sudden jerk and hurried after me down the stairs of the land yacht. "Wait! I'm coming too."

The door squealed shut behind him and we were alone on the pavement.

CHAPTER SIX

Wales is a Mysterious Place

I looked at Binky, astonished. "Why on Earth do you want to come along?"

"Our aunt frightens me. Besides you promised me dinner."

"Afraid you've missed dinner, Old Boy, but there may still be some cherries if we hurry. Are you sure you're up for this, Old Slipper?"

"No, but I'm protecting my interest. If I'm with you I can help you win that bet."

"Bravo. You are not quite the quivering panna cotta I took you for."

"Thanks very much, I'm sure."

"Now, what shall we call you?"

"Oh! Fun!" He staggered about a bit "um"ing and "er"ing then jerked to a stop. "Willie Whiffington-Charles!"

I eyed him doubtfully. "What about Dick?"

He looked as if he had smelled something distasteful. "What about it?"

"For a name. I'm Johny and you're Dick and we're from Wales."

"Why Wales?"

"Because no one knows anything about Wales. It's the most mysterious country on earth."

He gave a little sigh. "Fine. Dick. Hello, Dick. Have a drink, Dick. I suppose it will do."

"I'll introduce you as my cousin."

"I *am* your cousin."

"All the easier to keep our story straight. Hold on, we're getting close."

I pulled Binky into the shadows and scanned the building opposite us. "Cubby is in there somewhere keeping a beady eye on me. Can you pull your top over your head to hide your face?"

He wrestled with his burlap for a while. "How's that?"

With his shirt over his head, he looked rather like the Headless Horseman, but it would have to do.

"We'll hurry through the lobby. The apartment is up five flights of stairs."

His frightened eyes peered out from between his buttons. "And we have to climb them?"

"Don't be a baby. We'll stop when we have to."

I had built up some endurance already and we sped up the five flights in under an hour.

Ernie opened the door. "I'd about given up on you." He eyed Binky with alarm.

I winked broadly. "Would you believe it? I ran into my cousin Dick in the street! He's come from Wales as well! What a coincidence! It's Dick!"

Ernie was quick on the uptake. "So it is."

I leaned in and lowered my voice. "Can you manage it?"

"Of course. If we alternate sleeping head, toe, head we should all fit. Come on in." He herded us through the door. "Look who's back! And he's brought a friend."

His mum was busily washing dishes in the sink. "Hallo, Johny. Who's this?"

"This is my cousin.... Dick."

"Hello, Dick. Will you be staying with us?"

"If I may. It's very kind of you."

Ernie's mum shook a plate in our direction. "If we don't take care of each other the Corporate Overseers certainly won't."

Judy wandered over with what I had come to think of as The Sacred Bowl. "We saved you some cherries."

I turned to Binky. "Oh! Dick! Wait until you try them!"

Judy picked out a piece of fruit. "Here, open wide."

Binky popped open his mouth like a baby bird and she tossed it in.

"Careful. There's something hard in the middle. Don't swallow it," I warned him.

Judy looked at me askance. "That's called a pit. Have you really never eaten a cherry? Do they not grow in Wales?"

"Afraid not. The trade winds are too powerful. Blow them right off the trees."

Binky bit down. His eyes widened. He made a soft mewling sound.

"Quick, shove a chair under him!"

He dropped into the chair. His eyes rolled up in his head. I chafed his wrists. "I think he's fainted. No, he's all right."

His eyes opened. He stared into Judy's face as if he was having a holy vision. He carefully ejected the cherry pit into my proffered palm.

"What do you think?"

He held up a hand. "Give me a moment." His eyes focused on the middle distance. We all watched him with various levels of concern. Finally, he sighed. "No, it won't do. I shall have to re-evaluate all my beliefs."

Judy laughed. "I think he likes cherries."

Mum bustled up. "You enjoy them while we make up the beds. It's late."

"Is it?"

"We get up at six for work."

"By Jove! That will be a novelty."

"What time do you get up in Wales?"

"Noon. Sometimes later depending on the hangover."

Judy looked concerned. "It must be bad there if you have to drink to get through the day."

"Simply awful. That's why we came here, you know. To start fresh."

"Well, we'll help you in any way we can."

Binky gazed at her worshipfully. "Will you? What an extraordinary girl you are."

"Woman."

"Pardon?"

"Girl is a diminutive term. I'm a woman."

Binky gulped. "You certainly are."

She shook her head. "I don't suppose you're as evolved in Wales as we are here."

"No. Backwards sort of place. People blowing their noses in public and slapping each other on the back at all hours. Dreadful."

Mum returned to the kitchen area and gave the counter a final wipe. "Right. The beds are made. Dick and Johny, you'll crawl in with Ernie. Sleep well."

"Yes. I'm sure we will. Won't we, Dick?"

Binky was staring at the sleeping arrangements with horror. "I say..."

Ernie took us both by the elbow. "Dick, you take the side by the wall. I'll sleep head to toe in the middle and Johny can perch on the outer edge."

"What about pajamas?"

"Don't use 'em. Frivolous, aren't they?"

"So we just... sleep in our clothes?"

"You're welcome to sleep in the buff if you like. We'll hang a sheet up between us and the ladies."

"No. This will be fine."

Judy stood by the wall. "I'll get the light. Ready?" She turned down the gaslight, and the room was plunged into darkness.

The mattress was thin and lumpy. I lay on my back staring up into the black. I could hear the sounds of fellow creatures all around me—breathing, tossing, gently coughing. How I longed for one of Bentley's nighttime elixirs.

Ernie's feet lay between Binky and I emitting a sour, earthy smell.

"Sweet dreams, all."

"Night, Mum."

"Yes. Night."

"Indeed."

I twiddled my fingers and tried to pierce the darkness with my eyes. The jingle for "Dr. Pinochet's Foot Emporium" kept running through my head.

There was a rustle from Judy's corner. "Say Johny?"

"Yes?"

"Are you whistling?"

"Oh! I suppose I am. Sorry."

"Can't sleep?"

"Well, you know... new place and all."

"Aw, you're still homesick."

"I suppose that must be it."

There was a thoughtful pause. "What's it like in Wales?"

"Judy, leave him alone."

"Maybe talking about it will be good for him, Mum. Is it beautiful there?"

"Oh! Paradise! What with the... Welsh mountains towering over it all."

Binky propped himself on an elbow. "And the lonely moors stretching off into the distance."

"It sounds lovely."

"And the fjords of Wales, with their majestic glaciers."

"Really? Wales has glaciers?"

I gave Binky a poke. "Only in the Winter, of course."

Binky sat up. "As children we would frolic in the snow and eat ice cream scooped right out of the ice."

Ernie rolled over. "I don't think that's where ice cream comes from."

Judy's voice was dreamy. "Hush Ernie, he's being poetical."

I tried steering the conversation away from all things icy. "And then there's the people—finest in the world. Sturdy, rough-hewn, plain-spoken Welshmen."

"And Welsh women," Binky chimed in.

"Oh yes! The most beautiful in the world!"

Binky propped himself up on an elbow. "I disagree, Old Sloth. I think the women here are the loveliest I've ever seen."

I could hear the smile in Judy's voice. "Well, Dick! Do you have your eye on someone special?"

"I do, but alas, I fear she doesn't know I exist."

"Then you should tell her. Women aren't mind readers, you know."

I raised an eyebrow. "Really? They certainly seem to anticipate *my* every move."

"Hush now. It'll be a new day before you know it."

"But I'm not the least bit sleepy, Mum. Say, Dick, what are the politics like in Wales? Is there a resistance?"

"A resistance to what?"

"To things as they are. Business as usual. The oppression of the masses."

Binky wrapped his arms around his knees and began rocking back and forth. "Oh yes! We've got a cracking resistance. Many's the time my friends and I have met over a drink to point out the shortcomings of the local administration."

"But what action are you taking?"

"Action?"

"To change things. To redistribute wealth. To break the power of the monopolies. To create meaningful jobs."

Binky began rocking faster. "Well, it's funny you should bring that up. I was just saying to my friends in the Welsh Underground that we've got to shake things up, don't you know, in a major way."

"By doing what?"

"Well... you know... I've been formulating a plan, but it's top secret. Can't breathe a word of it, but it's a corker."

"So, you are one of the leaders of your movement?"

"Well, I don't like to brag but... some people call me... The Welsh Rabbit, because I'm so bally elusive, don't you know."

"Really?"

This was going rather too far. "Perhaps you should put a sock in it and go to sleep, Old Rabbit, before you reveal anything top secret."

"Yes, perhaps we all should try to get some rest."

"Sorry, Mum. We'll talk more tomorrow, Dick. There are some people I want to introduce you to."

"Only too happy... any friend of yours, etcetera. Looking forward to it."

"That's enough now."

"Good night, Mum."

I carefully slid my head over as close to Binky as I could. This, unfortunately brought me smack up against Ernie's fragrant feet. Breathing through my mouth I whispered in Binky's ear.

"Now you've done it, you dunderhead! Why couldn't you keep quiet?"

"I couldn't help it. Isn't she wonderful?"

"Who?"

"Judy! I think she's the loveliest girl I've ever seen. Do you think I have a chance?"

"No! By no means. Absolutely not. Put it out of your head entirely."

"I think I do. I detected a certain note in her voice when she spoke of financial redistribution that was almost tender."

"Will you, for the love of all that's holy, go to sleep?"

"Good night, Cyril. I mean Johny!"

"Good night!"

And with that I moved as far away from Ernie's feet as possible and tried to imagine myself in my silk sheets at home with a brandy on the night stand and the soothing sounds of Bentley oiling his gears in the moonlight.

CHAPTER SEVEN

I Get a Job

I'm sure that in Heaven one is awakened each morning by the aroma of pancakes. There is no surer proof of the Divine Being than this: He brought forth pancakes on the earth. I practically levitated out of the communal bed—not minding at all that the sun was barely up. At the stove, Ernie's mother was performing the sort of alchemy that would have led her to the stake in less enlightened times.

"Morning everyone. There's pancakes with syrup, fried potatoes with onions and peppers, and hot rolls with jam."

Binky's eyes were like saucers. "What is happening? I feel like a child on Christmas morning."

I gave him a nudge in the rib cage. "This is the grub I was telling you about. Wait until you taste it!"

Ernie waved from the other side of the room. "The sink is free. Johny, do you need to borrow a toothbrush?"

"Hang on." I checked my pockets and found that Bentley had foreseen everything. A toothbrush and paste lay in a clever inner pocket. "Got one."

Binky was looking at my toothbrush wistfully. "Could I borrow it when you're through?"

"Certainly not. Unhygienic."

"May I use some paste? I can put it on my finger."

"I suppose. You really should have come better prepared."

"I expected to be staying with Cheeseworth."

"Shh! Keep your voice down. Here's the paste. Have at it."

In a matter of minutes we were brushed, scrubbed and seated at the table. Platters of pancakes, bowls of potatoes, baskets of rolls! I loaded up my plate and paused to watch Binky take his first bite. He did not disappoint. One bite of pancake and the fork fell from his nerveless fingers. He rose shakily to his feet and paced from one end of the apartment to the other. Ernie watched him with concern.

"Everything all right, Dick?"

I gave his arm a reassuring pat. "He's never had pancakes before... not really."

"Wales must be a dismal place."

"Yes, we mostly dine on thistles."

Binky finally seated himself, took a deep breath and proceeded to shovel food into his maw with an industry I had never suspected him capable of. I eyed him with concern.

"Steady, my lad. It's customary to chew the food before swallowing it. You're not an anaconda, after all."

Judy brought another stack of pancakes. "After we eat, we'll head over to the tax office. I'll get chits for you and Dick to wait in line and then I'm going to round up the friends I wanted you to meet."

"That sounds perfect."

Binky had nearly reached the top of his digestive tract and was laying on a spackle coat for good measure. He groaned and patted his stomach. "I must say... that was the most incredible meal of my life. Bravo!"

Mum blushed a little. "It's nice to be appreciated. I must do something special for dinner if I'm to have an audience like this."

"Oh yes, please! I shall count the hours."

Judy shoved back her chair. "Come on, everybody. Off we go."

Ernie grabbed his jacket. "I've got to make my grocery deliveries. I'll see you all later."

I seized him by the cuff. "Ernie, a word in your ear." We strolled to the far end of the room. "Will you be seeing Bentley today?"

"Yes. I'm delivering a load of Mrs. Cumber's beefy and mushroomy pies."

"No beef in them, I suppose?"

"Certainly not, nor mushrooms!"

"All right, cancel that order, then go to the house and apprise Bentley of our progress so far... and ask him for a toothbrush for Binky so he'll stop pestering me."

"Got it."

"Thanks awfully."

We strode back to join the others—a journey of no more than ten feet. "Here's to an honest day's work, everyone!"

Judy looked at me askance. "Sure. I guess."

"Sorry. I'm a little overstimulated by all the syrup."

We followed Judy down the stairs and through the morning crowd of workers milling on the street. I got a jolt when I spotted the beetle-browed Cubby Martinez lounging under a nearby awning. He waited for us to pass him, then casually began tailing us from about a block back. I drew up next to Binky and murmured into his ear, "Don't look back, but Cubby Martinez is on our trail."

I felt him stiffen, but to his credit he resisted the urge to spin around and gawk. "What shall we do?"

"Nothing for it but to play our parts. He's got to see the others treating us as equals or the bet's as good as lost."

"Got it."

As we passed through a large square filled with people, an oily-looking fellow jumped up on an apple box and began to orate. "Ladies and Gentlemen! Do you suffer from lethargy, dry skin, flatulence or halitosis? Try Bean's Specific—the tonic..."

Before we could get more details about Bean's Specific, the speaker was drowned in a chorus of catcalls and showered with loose pieces of pavement. He grabbed his apple box and ran for his life. I turned to Judy in astonishment.

"I say, what was all that about?"

Judy tossed a final rock in his direction and brushed her hands. "Advertisement. We don't stand for 'em. Propaganda from the ruling class designed to make us discontented and divided. He's lucky he got off with a few pebbles."

"I always thought of ads as public service announcements."

"Don't you believe it—insidious things... brainwashing. You won't find them around here."

"This is highly educational, I must say."

There was a rumble that grew steadily louder. Judy grabbed my arm and pulled me up against the nearest building as a steam-powered Hawaiian war canoe shot around the corner. Standing by the steering paddle was my old friend, Ford. I lowered my face to avoid detection. People leaped out of his path, screaming and shaking their fists. An errant oar smashed into a fruit stand, scattering apples everywhere. Ford shot around another corner and something like peace returned to the street. The fruit seller sadly collected his apples—which were now somewhat the worse for wear.

"Of all the gall! These rich idiots with their ridiculous transports. Did you see him? He couldn't have cared less about the mayhem he left behind him."

I must confess, my thoughts turned to my own history of careening through the streets in vehicles ranging from a chariot to a three-masted galleon. I found that my recollections, rather than being fond, were now tinged with shame. I resolved to drive more carefully in future and

managed to regain my equanimity. A short time later we came to a dreary monolith of a building

with the moniker "Bureau of Taxes" printed on it. A line of grim-looking townsfolk snaked out of the doorway and down the block. Cubby parked himself within earshot and tried to look inconspicuous. Judy led us to the end of the line.

"This is us. That's my supervisor over there. Oy, Martha!"

A sturdy looking woman trundled up. "Hallo, Judy. This the Welshman you told me about?"

"Yes. His cousin Dick showed up too. Have you got room for him?"

"Absolutely. Crazy day."

She checked her clipboard and tore off two chits. "All right, which of you is Johny?"

"That's me."

She handed me the chit. "You're waiting for Pete. Dick, you're waiting for Nancy. Don't leave the line for any reason. When Pete and Nancy show up, give them these chits and let them take your place in line. Simple enough?"

"Got it."

"Absolutely."

"I'll be by now and then to check on you. Good luck."

Martha moved on to new arrivals. The line grew rapidly behind us.

I looked about eagerly. "So! This is a job! We're working. Productive members of society. It's rather thrilling."

Judy grimaced. "Say that again five hours from now. Move your weight from foot to foot. Keeps the blood from pooling."

At that moment, to my horror, I spied my aunt and uncle strolling through the crowd followed by Cheeseworth, who was carrying a splintered branch in place of his usual walking stick. They gawked at the locals like the worst kinds of tourists. If Cubby saw them with me the game was up. He was lounging nearby keeping us within his peripheral vision. I pointed at him theatrically. "I say, who's that suspicious-looking fellow lurking over there?"

"Where?"

"That hirsute fellow with his hands in his pockets. I believe he's about to start an advertisement!"

Judy frowned at Cubby. "Oh, is he? Oy! You!"

Cubby spun around to find the entire line staring at him.

Judy put her hands on her hips. "What's your business here?"

Cubby gave a supercilious sniff. "Who, me?"

"Yes you. Are you advertising something?"

"No! I'm simply standing here."

"Nobody just stands anywhere unless they're an advertisement or a spy for the corporations. Are you a spy?"

"Certainly not, madam."

"Madam! That's pretty fancy talk for someone who's just standing there. You'd better clear out before we clear you out, get it?"

Cubby sputtered. "Now see here..."

"All right, everybody, let's help him on his way!"

And before you could say "boo," a crowd of sturdy citizenry had picked Cubby up by the arms and run him down the street.

Judy gave a satisfied grunt. "That's fixed him."

"Yoo-hoo! Johny!"

Just in the nick of time. The gaggle of relations had arrived!

CHAPTER EIGHT

A Tangled Web

My aunt waved at me gaily. "What a coincidence, running into you like this."

"Yes, Aunt!" I jerked my elbow at Binky and waggled my eyebrows. "You remember Dick!"

Binky raised his hand. "That's me. I'm Dick."

My aunt winked at us knowingly. "So you are. And I am your Aunt... er... Lucretia... and your Uncle is, of course... Mortimer."

Uncle Hugo reddened. "Oh, blast!"

I stepped aside and gestured. "This is Judy. It's her family we're staying with."

Judy shoved out a flipper. "Hallo."

My aunt grasped the offered appendage. "A pleasure. What a pretty thing you are. Like a squashed rosebud or a fallen begonia."

Judy squinted at her. "I guess... thanks?"

"It shows that beauty can be found anywhere. Even the oily scum on a waste containment pond holds a rainbow... if the angle of the sun is right."

I wagged a thumb at Cheeseworth, who was fumbling for his non-existent monocle.

"Aunt, who is your friend? The one inexplicably carrying a length of tree?"

"This is..."

Cheeseworth spoke in a low rasp. "Caligula. My name is Caligula, as you know, of course, from our long years of acquaintance."

"Of course! Caligula! Didn't recognize you with the sun in my eyes."

Judy turned to Aunt Hypatia. "You're all from Wales?"

"Are we?" My aunt squinted at me and considered for a moment. "We are."

I put an arm around her to keep her from wandering into traffic. "All of us Welsh to the core. But what are you doing here, Aunt?"

I realized my mistake at once. She had not troubled to prepare a back story. When discomfited, my aunt can form herself into a sort of walled fortress. She planted herself firmly and gazed down at me from the battlements.

"What do you suppose?"

Binky couldn't resist a guessing game. "What fun! Let's see... did something happen at home?"

My aunt turned to him eagerly. "That sounds promising."

"Was it... a disaster of some sort?"

"Excellent. Continue in that vein."

"Perhaps... a famine of some kind?"

She smiled triumphantly. "That seems credible. Yes, we are fleeing a famine."

Judy clucked sympathetically. "Was it a lack of rainfall?"

"Locusts," Cheeseworth intoned solemnly.

"Locusts?"

"Devoured everything. Wholesale starvation. All the Welsh had to flee."

Judy whistled. "All the Welsh?"

"Well, you know the population was never very large," I assured her. "The Welsh are noted for their lackadaisical attitude toward procreation."

"What a strange place Wales must be. Look here, do you need jobs?"

My aunt brightened. "I suppose we must. Mortimer, do we need jobs?"

"I would rather starve."

She glared at him. "Foolish Welsh pride. It will be the death of him if I do not kill him first myself. We came here to experience everything and menial labor is certainly part of the fun."

Cheeseworth cackled. "Oh indeed! I can hardly wait to tell our fwiends... in Wales, about our adventures."

My aunt looked around eagerly. "What would these jobs entail?"

"You just have to wait in line. Oy! Martha!"

Martha strode over. "What's up?"

"I've got three more for you."

"Fine. I've got chits for Sam, Helen and Paul. Who wants who?"

Judy handed out the chits. "Here, Lucretia, you take Sam; Mortimer you're Helen, and Caligula you're Paul.

Aunt Hypatia examined her chit. "In what manner are we connected to these individuals?"

"You're holding their places in line."

"We seem eminently qualified for such an activity."

Cheeseworth looked around at the line. "So, as of this moment, we are working?"

"You are. You'll be paid by the hour starting now."

"How thwilling."

I noticed some dark glares from the people in line behind us and heard grumblings of "We were here before they were. They should go to the back of the line. It's against the rules." And so on.

My aunt was having none of it. "Silence! I will not be bullied by a pack of nit-picking, rule quoting complainers. Who do you think you are? Stop it at once!"

There were sheepish murmurings of "Sorry, Ma'am. We didn't mean any harm." Apparently, Aunt Hypatia's powers crossed all boundaries of age, sex and social standing.

I cleared my throat. "So, Aunt... hm..."

"Lucretia."

"I know! Of course I know. So, Aunt Lucretia, what have you been up to this morning?"

"Taking in the sights, you know. It's so colorful—people running here and there. Stands selling knitted garments and foodstuffs. Have you ever heard of a churro?"

"Can't say I have."

"It is a kind of edible. Cylindrical, with ridges."

"Did you try one?"

"Certainly not! Who knows what lurks beneath their enticing golden crust?"

Judy's head had been bobbing back and forth following the conversation. "It's just fried dough with sugar and cinnamon."

"There, you see? Cinnamon—a most sinister word."

I sighed. "I wish you would try some of the food here, Aunt. It really is extraordinary."

"That's as may be. I believe that if something is pleasurable it is merely a gateway to more unbridled behavior and who knows where it will all end?"

"When I find out I will let you know."

She looked around impatiently. "Well, this has been no end of fun. When does this Sam person arrive?"

"It will be hours yet," answered Judy.

"Oh, I don't think so."

"Yes, Aunt. This is 'work.' It's not supposed to be fun, you know."

"Then why do it?"

Judy looked puzzled. "For money... in order to live. Don't you work in Wales?"

I gave my aunt a warning glance. "I'm afraid the work ethic there is not what it is here."

Cheeseworth leaned on his branch. "And of course there are the locusts, with their vowacious jaws and segmented carapaces."

Judy shook her head. "Well, we work here. You have to—unless you want to live on nutrition bars and water."

My uncle looked affronted. "What's wrong with nutrition bars?"

"Do you like them?"

"I have never tried one."

Judy clapped her hands. "What? Have you got a treat coming. Oy! Who's got a nutrition bar they can spare?"

There was some hubbub in the crowd and a voice sang out. "Here you go. Fizzy Berry Blast."

The bar was passed from hand to hand until it reached Uncle Hugo. He peeled back the wrapper and regarded it dubiously. "It looks inoffensive enough. Rather gelatinous."

Judy watched him with a smile. "Go on. Don't be afraid."

He took a nibble and chewed delicately. "Hmm." Suddenly the flavour hit him. He gagged and slapped at his tongue. "Good God! That is absolutely horrible! Like a cross between a rotting banana and turpentine!"

"Could you live on those?"

"No. I admit it. I could not."

My uncle carefully deposited the slimy remains in a nearby rubbish bin and wiped at his tongue with his sleeve.

Judy spotted a small group passing by. "Sid! Over here! This is lucky, I was just going to look for you."

The group came over, led by a rather dashing young fellow with a mustache.

"Hello, Judy."

Judy pulled Binky over by the sleeve. "Dick, these are the folks I was telling you about. Friends, meet the Welsh Rabbit."

They all stared at Binky.

"The Welsh what?"

"Rabbit, on account of he's so hard to catch. He's a top member of the Welsh underground."

Sid stuck out his hand. "Is he? Glad to meet you, Rabbit."

Binky dug a toe into the dirt. "Judy is exaggerating my importance..."

"Don't be modest. He has some big plans to shake things up in Wales."

"As soon as the locusts depart," Cheeseworth added.

I gave him a surreptitious nudge. "You really are fixated on those locusts, Caligula."

"I was twapped in a locust swarm in younger days. I am haunted by the sounds of their chewing to this day."

Judy turned back to Sid. "What are you all up to?"

"We've just been talking about how to break the power of the local monopoly."

"What monopoly is that," I inquired innocently.

"Smythe Corporation, of course."

My uncle spun around. "Did you say, Smythe Corporation?"

"They're evil, I tell you... predatory. And it's all owned by one man—that Chippington-Smythe monster."

This seemed a tad beyond the pale. "I've heard he's not so bad."

"Don't you believe it! He's the richest man on the planet and look how he treats us—buys up all the land to plant soybeans that we're not allowed to eat. Gives all the best jobs to robots. Crams birth control in our Fizzy Berry Blast Bars."

The colour drained from my uncle's face. "What, in that thing I just bit into?"

Aunt Hypatia snorted. "You need hardly worry about birth control, Mortimer. Not while I am alive."

I stepped up to Sid. "Look, I happen to know that this Chippington-Smythe fellow didn't know about any of it."

"He's just an unwitting tool," chirped Binky.

"A well-meaning idiot."

"Yes, thank you, Uncle."

Judy frowned. "But how do you know this?"

It was out before I could think of a better story line. "Well... as it happens, through a strange quirk of fate, I'm... acquainted with the fellow."

She stared at me. "You know Cyril Chippington-Smythe?"

"Yes, and I can tell you he's not the monster you take him for. Why, I believe that when he finds out about all the things that have been done in his name he won't rest until he's put them right."

Judy looked dubious. "Do you really believe that?"

"I do."

"Then you've got to tell him."

"Who, me?"

"You said you knew him."

My aunt gave a little cough. "They are intimately acquainted."

"Do you know where he lives?"

Binky giggled. "Of course he does."

"Then let's go there now."

"Right this minute?"

"Why not?"

"What if he's... in the shower?"

"Then we'll wait. This is too great an opportunity to miss. Oy! Martha!"

"What's up?"

"Emergency. We'll have to turn over our chits."

"All right. I'll take them to the back of the line. See you tomorrow."

Judy raised a fist. "Come on, everybody. We're off to see Cyril Chippington-Smythe! Three cheers for Johny! Hip hip..."

"Hooray!"

"Hip hip..."

"Hooray!"

"Hip hip..."

"Hooray!"

And with that they lifted me onto their shoulders and began to jog down the street with Binky pointing the way and my relations bringing up the rear. This was a hornet's nest and no mistake. In my despair I clung to one ray of hope. Each step was bringing us closer to Bentley. If anyone could find a way to oil out from under this mess it was he. I lay back on the sea of hands that supported me, gazed up at the fluffy clouds above me and surrendered myself to the vagaries of fortune.

CHAPTER NINE

My Short but Brilliant Acting Career

Though I present an elegant figure to the world, I am heavier than I look. The fun of carrying me on their shoulders soon palled and after a few blocks I was set on my feet. With each stride carrying me closer to home and almost certain discovery, I wracked my brains for an escape plan. Sid walked up next to me.

"What's this Chippington-Smythe fellow like? We've never seen him."

"Well... people say he's rather good-looking."

Binky slipped in between us. "Are you sure about that? I've heard he has a somewhat mouse-like flavour."

"And a hunchback fwom a bout of childhood scoliosis," snickered Cheeseworth.

I regarded them coldly. "Not at all. He is known for the strength of his profile and the grace of his calves."

Sid gave me an odd look. "Well, you certainly admire him."

"He is a gentleman. I think that sums him up."

Judy harrumphed. "It's gentlemen that have got the world in this state. We don't think much of gentlemen."

"Would you have the world run by a ragtag mob of illiterates?" asked Uncle Hugo.

"Steady, Mortimer. If we're ragtag it's because they haven't left us the means to dress any better, and a fancy education obviously doesn't produce a superior product."

My aunt chortled. "She's slapped you on the snout rather soundly Mortimer. Bravo, young Judy."

Sid sidled over to us. "Should we talk about our list of demands?"

This seemed like a promising diversion. "Yes! Why don't we go somewhere and discuss it at length. We can always come back tomorrow... or next week."

Judy shook her head firmly. "No, we've got to strike while the iron is hot."

Sid stroked his mustache. "We should be on our guard. This fellow is an evil genius, after all."

"Perhaps he's only an idiot savant," I murmured weakly.

"That's half right," said Uncle Hugo.

We trudged on—past empty buildings and soybean fields. The sun beat down and morale began to flag.

Judy looked around. "Say, Rabbit. Tell us about the Welsh Underground."

There was a pause as Binky, lost in his thoughts, tried to make a whistle out of a blade of grass.

I poked him, hard, in the ribs. "I say, Rabbit! They're talking to you."

"What? Oh, me! I'm the Rabbit."

I smiled at Judy. "He's trained not to react to his code name, you see. In case the authorities try to trip him up."

"Pretty good. He fooled me."

"They want you to tell them about the Underground," I said to Binky, a little too loudly.

My aunt looked thoughtful. "I have never understood the subterranean reference. It conjures up images of dirt and burrowing insects. Who would join such an organization? They would have done much better to associate it with a woodland glade. Or the seashore."

Binky shook his head. "You can't plan an insurrection at the seashore—with the waves crashing and the wind blowing. You can't hear yourself think."

"Yes, that's true. I withdraw the seashore."

Sid was struggling to keep up. "But what has the Welsh Underground been doing?"

I could see that Binky was enjoying himself. Anything that smacked of theatrical improvisation was catnip to him. "Oh! We've got scads of plans. There's the Spring fund-raiser coming up, and we're designing uniforms..."

Judy turned to him. "You can't wear uniforms if you're in the underground! They'll know who you are."

"Oh! Right! The uniforms are for after... after we overthrow the oppressors. There's sure to be a parade and won't we look smart in our matching outfits?"

"You must be pretty confident."

"Well, the government's as rotten as an old log. One good push and down it will come."

"So, what's the push going to be?"

"Specifically?"

"Can you not talk about it?"

"Only in general terms."

Cheeseworth leaned in curiously. "Does it have anything to do with locusts and their incessant stridulations?"

"I don't think so. No, when it happens, you'll hear about it. It's going to be positively explosive."

Judy recoiled a little. "Explosive? That's pretty hardcore. We were only talking about going on strike."

"What? Oh, I didn't mean..."

"Maybe we shouldn't talk about it anymore. We don't want to be accessories to anything."

Aunt Hypatia, whose attention had wandered, perked up at this. "You can never have too many accessories, in my opinion. They add a *'je ne sais quoi'* to any ensemble."

We rounded a corner and there stood the ancestral manse. I had always found it warm and inviting, but with that angry mob milling about, it only wanted some heads on pikes and hungry ravens to resemble a medieval fortress. Judy rang the doorbell.

I giggled nervously. "Probably not home. Gone to the country no doubt. Oh well."

The door opened and Bentley stood before us. His optical sensors scanned the crowd and settled on me. I could hear his gears working.

Judy stepped forth. "Good morning."

"Good morning, Miss."

"Is Mr. Chippington-Smythe at home?"

Bentley gazed at me with no expression whatsoever. "I believe he is, Miss."

"Tell him his old friend Johny is here to see him."

I jumped to the front of the line. "Yes! Hello... Bentley, is it? Good to see you again. How've you been?"

"I am well, Sir."

"When my friends here found out I knew Mr. Chippington-Smythe they insisted we come and chat him up. Run some ideas by him, you know... about social change and all that."

"Indeed, Sir? I'm sure he will find it most enlightening."

I worked the old eyebrows at him. "But he's probably busy, eh? Couldn't possibly spare the time, no doubt?"

"On the contrary. Mr. Chippington-Smythe is at leisure. Allow me to show you to the parlour. Please come in, everyone."

Well, I couldn't imagine what Bentley was playing at. I'd given him an opening and he'd muffed it. I led the mob into the house and we pooled in the parlour by the sliding panels which separated it from my den. Bentley parked himself in front of the doors.

"I'm afraid I must insist that Mr. Chippington-Smythe speak with Johny alone. He is rather eccentric and is terrified of crowds."

I stared at him icily. "Oh, eccentric is he?"

"Extremely. If you would accompany me through the doors Mr. Chippington-Smythe will meet with you now."

Judy took my hand. "It's on you, Johny. You've got to speak for all of us."

I gave her fingers a squeeze. "Never fear. He shall feel my righteous indignation."

Bentley slid the doors open just wide enough for me to sidle through and followed me in, closing the doors behind us.

I whirled on him and whispered hoarsely. "What the devil are you playing at, Bentley?"

He was unperturbed. "May I ask how your adventure is progressing, Sir?"

"We're in the soup! That's how it's progressing."

"Have your opinions about the poor been altered by your experiences?"

I leaned against a table and hung my head. "Have they! Bentley, my eyes have been opened. Do you know, I'm not sure I don't want to hang this Chippington-Smythe myself. My company has done terrible things. In spite of all of it, the people thrive. Their lives are infinitely more interesting than ours. And the food! Bentley, you'll have to throw away everything in the larder. No more manufactured ersatz anything. From now on it's fresh food for me."

"I am gratified to hear it, Sir."

"Did Ernie come by? I told him to update you."

"Yes, Sir. We had an extensive conversation. He is a remarkable young man."

"His sister is a firecracker—full of ideas about social justice. And his mum is a chef of the first magnitude."

"It's a pity that their gifts are not being fully utilized."

"That's so true."

"Perhaps you could alter their situations, Sir."

"Who, me?"

"If not you, then who? If not now, when?"

"Oh! I love riddles. Let's see... if not you..."

He sighed. "Perhaps we should leave that for another time."

"Yes. Now how do I get out of this mess?"

Bentley's gears began chugging away. A tiny jet of steam puffed from his right ear. "I suggest what might be referred to as a theatrical ploy. If you alter your voice to play the role of Mr.

Chippington-Smythe you can hold a conversation with yourself as "Johny" that will be overheard in the parlour. One voice will make demands, the other will acquiesce and your friends need never lay eyes on the mysterious owner of the Smythe Corporation."

"By Jove! It's genius. How do you think this monster should speak?" I growled in a rather piratical manner. "See here, my lad, if you think you can just walk in here..."

"A bit stereotypical, Sir."

"What about this?" I went up the octave and added a simper. "Oh, Johny, thank goodness you brought this to my attention. You know what a hopeless idiot I am."

"Again, Sir, I believe a lighter hand is called for."

"Fine. I say, Johny, those are some rather good points you're making."

"That is acceptable, Sir."

I began pacing with a rolling gait. "Now, how should he walk?"

Bentley gave another small sigh. "Tempus fugit, Sir."

"Yes, yes. Here we go."

I began loudly as Johny. "Now look here, Chippington-Smythe, these kinds of business practices just won't wash! These aren't the dark ages, you know."

I switched voices and turned my body to face the other way. "Why, what on earth do you mean, Old Bag?"

I switched again. "You're oppressing the poor, you know."

"Am I? I had no idea!

"Well, that's all right, my lad. I'm here to set it right. You just listen to old Johny and we'll soon have this place running like a clock."

"Oh, Johny! Thank goodness for you! I bless the day that we became fast friends."

"Yes, friendship like ours can't be bought at any price."

"I say, have you lost weight?"

"A pound or two. Can you tell?"

"Oh yes! You're lean as an athlete. I'm sure you could enter the Olympics if you cared about such things."

"For that matter, you're looking rather dashing yourself. Have you done something different with your hair?"

Bentley cleared his throat. I hurriedly finished up.

"Well, never mind about that, Johny. What should I do about all this social injustice and whatnot?"

"I'll tell you exactly what to do..."

Bentley held up his hand. "That should be sufficient, Sir. If you could lower your voice and murmur unintelligibly for a few moments, I believe we can conclude our masquerade."

I followed instructions. "Rada-frazza-upsilon. Oopsy daisy Allegheny Monongahela."

"And now I believe you may rejoin your guests, Sir."

CHAPTER TEN

Many Surprises

Bentley slid open the pocket doors and we squeezed through, shutting them behind us.

Judy rushed up to me. "Well? What did he say?"

"He's an amazing chap, I must say. Mind like a razor. Chin of granite."

"But what did he say?"

"Oh, he's all for reform. Said yes to everything."

"But what, specifically?"

"Well, we didn't have time to go into all the details."

Judy exhaled loudly. "Then, what did you achieve?"

Bentley stepped up. "I'm afraid Johny is too modest to boast of his accomplishments. If I may clarify what actually took place—Mr.

Chippington-Smythe agreed to the creation of a new position within the company—answerable only to him and empowered to make any changes that might improve the lives of the general population. These would include but are not limited to: the areas of job creation, better housing and land redistribution. That's correct, isn't it, Sir?"

"Oh! Yes. That's just what we decided."

Judy snorted. "Corporate mumbo-jumbo."

Bentley continued. "And Johny insisted that this position be filled by someone who could indisputably be trusted to act in the best interests of the people."

"Who's that going to be?"

Bentley turned to me. "Did you want to be the one to tell her, Sir?"

"Who, me?"

"It was your idea, after all."

"Oh! Yes. It was my idea. Wouldn't have had it any other way."

Judy stared at me expectantly. "Who is it?"

"It's..." I goggled at Bentley but he just looked back at me like a schoolmaster surveying a particularly dull specimen. Suddenly the light dawned. "You, Judy!" I glanced at Bentley. "That's right, isn't it?"

"Absolutely correct."

"Got it in one go."

Judy's jaw was hanging open. "Me?"

"Of course. Who else?"

Sid raised her hand in the air. "Three cheers for Judy! Hip hip..."

"Hooray!"

"Hip hip..."

"Hooray!"

"Hip hip..."

"Hooray!"

Uncle Hugo was turning purple. "The government will never accept it!"

I looked at him thoughtfully. "But Smythe Corporation owns the government, doesn't it?"

He huffed and puffed for a while and finally looked down at his shoes. "Not officially."

"But for all intents and purposes."

"Well... off the record, yes."

"Then that's taken care of."

He shook his fist. "But what of the shareholders?"

"What of the shareholders indeed?"

Bentley glided in. "I think you will find, as Mr. Chippington-Smythe expressed it, that a rising tide lifts all boats. After all, if people have money to spend, they become customers—and since

Smythe Corporation sells virtually everything, business should thrive."

Uncle Hugo's hue became less crimson. He looked thoughtful. "So, the money lost in soybean subsidies will be made up in consumer goods. Brilliant!"

At that moment there was a slam from the front door followed by a flurry of pounding feet and a hyperventilating Cubby Martinez burst into the room. He stared about him with wild eyes and pointed an accusatory finger at me. "Ah hah! The evidence could not be clearer. I declare the wager lost!"

Judy squinted at Cubby. "Who the Hell are you? Say, you're that ad man from outside the tax office."

"I am Cubby Martinez, the Marshall of Twits."

"The what of what?"

I gave him a warning stare. "Look here, Cubby, you've got this all wrong."

"You won't talk your way out this time."

"Cubby, if you'll just turn around and leave, I'll explain it all to you later."

"Too late. Clearly these people know who you are."

Judy stared at me, then at Cubby. "Who is he?"

"He is Cyril Chippington-Smythe, of course, who has finally gotten his comeuppance."

"He's who?"

Cubby gave a grim laugh. "Chippington-Smythe here wagered that he could live like a common citizen for one week. If his identity was discovered the bet was lost, and here you all are—in his very house!"

At this point Bentley gave a little cough. "Excuse me, Sir. If I understand the terms of the wager, there was another codicil which stated that if his identity was revealed prematurely through some blunder on your part, Mr. Chippington-Smythe was to be declared the winner."

"What of it?"

Bentley looked around. "Prior to the entrance of Mr. Martinez, did anyone here suspect that this gentleman was anything other than a common citizen named Johny?"

There was a general chorus of, "Not me. Did you? No, I never!"

Sid shook his head. "He certainly fooled us."

Cubby's mouth opened and closed like a fish who suddenly finds the water has disappeared. "But... but..."

Uncle Hugo pointed a finger between Cubby's eyes. "I can attest that those are the facts, and I believe my word is good at the club."

Aunt Hypatia fixed Cubby with her basilisk's glare. "I too can verify that my nephew had become indistinguishable from a member of the working class until your untimely intervention and I would like to see any member of your club contradict me."

Binky was practically dancing. "Hooray! We're saved! You've really put your foot in it, Cubby. Wait until I tell the fellows. My bar tab in the new year is going to be monstrous!"

Cubby had grown progressively redder and seemed to be shrinking before my eyes. Finally, with a shriek like a steam whistle, he spun and ran from the room.

I gave a shrug. "Well, that seems to be that."

Judy stepped in front of me. "Not quite. There's still the little matter of who you are."

I hung my head. "Oh. Yes. I'm terribly sorry about that."

"Are you really Cyril Chippington-Smythe?"

"I'm afraid so."

"And there is no Johny?"

"He was an avatar, if you will."

She smiled sadly. "Pity. I rather liked him." She turned to Binky. "And I suppose you're not a feared member of the Welsh resistance?"

"Um... no, sorry. The truth is I have no resistance of any kind."

"There is no Welsh Rabbit?"

I chuckled. "He was called "Rabbit" at school, but it derived from a gentle nature and a habitual twitch of the nose rather than from any elusiveness."

Binky dropped to a knee. "Can you forgive me?"

Judy looked down at him. "Will you promise to tell me the absolute truth in future?"

"I do. Whenever I am able to discern it. Slippery thing—truth."

"It's enough that you try. I think we can remain friends."

Aunt Hypatia looked around with satisfaction. "I must say, this 'slumming' has turned out to be a great success. I almost regret not sampling that churro... but regrets, like influenza, are a part of life."

To my surprise, Ernie came strolling in from the direction of the kitchen. "Hello, all."

"Ernie! What are you doing here?"

"I had to make sure Mr. Martinez got here all right."

"*You* sent Cubby here?"

"I was in the kitchen making my delivery when Bentley saw the crowd coming. He sent me on the double to find Cubby and make sure he knew what was going on."

I turned to Bentley. "Once again it seems that it was Bentley's invisible hand moving us all about like chess pieces."

"You give me far too much credit, Sir."

I turned back to Ernie. "Say, listen, Ernie. As long as I'm creating new jobs, I've got one for you."

"What is it?"

"You're the new head of research at Smythe Corporation. You'll have everything you need—lab, assistants, equipment. Now you can find that 'fizzy energy' you've been looking for."

He grabbed my hand and shook it. "Do you mean it? Hooray!"

"And I've got a job for your mum as well, if she wants it. Do you think she'd be interested in cooking for me?"

"Full time, you mean?"

"At a generous salary with benefits of course."

Bentley gave a little bow. "I anticipated your interest, Sir. She is in the kitchen as we speak. I took the liberty of placing the auto-cooker in the trash."

My aunt gave a sniff. "This house begins to feel more like a pleasure palace than a respectable home. I am not quite sure how I feel about it, so I'm afraid I must disapprove until I have more information."

Ernie's mum entered the room, pushing a tea cart with platters of delicious-looking bits of this and that. "Hallo, everybody. I've thrown together some hors d'oeuvres. Is anyone hungry?"

The crowd headed for the cart with cries of "Yes! I am. Save some for me."

"There's eggplant dip, roasted peppers and warm flatbread with olive oil."

Aunt Hypatia threw her ragged shawl around her shoulders like an empress. "That settles it. Come, Hugo. An orgy seems to be breaking out and I do not wish to be listed among the participants."

I bowed her to the door. "Goodbye, Aunt. Do visit again soon."

"I shall not cross this threshold again until you've come to your senses."

"That's all right then. See you at Christmas."

She and my uncle sailed out of the door.

Cheeseworth hurried up an gave me an apologetic look. "Sowwy, Cywil. They're my ride. Toodle-oo."

I firmly shut the door then made a beeline for the flatbread. I drew Ernie's mum aside. "Look here, are you sure you want to work for a bloodsucking capitalist?"

She smiled. "You were a bloodsucking capitalist when I didn't know you. You're family now, which means your bloodsucking capitalism is only an endearing eccentricity. Besides, the job comes with dental."

"I say, I've never found out your name. I can't very well go on calling you Ernie's mum."

"It's Cook."

"Cook?"

"Short for Cookie. My parents were somewhat whimsical with names. My siblings are Brownie, Clementine and Potato."

"Cook, then. Perfect."

And so ended my adventure into the wide world. Later that evening I sat contentedly before my hydrogen gas fireplace sipping a cherry juice with soda and munching on a plate of toast and jam. With my girdle safely around my waist once more, I felt snug as the proverbial insect in the carpet. Bentley floated in.

"Cook is leaving for the evening, Sir."

"I wish you could taste her toast and jam."

"Alas, I lack the necessary sensors. Your adventure seems to have turned out rather well, if I may say so."

"I feel this is the beginning of a new age. An age of... toast, you know... and jam and such." I looked up at him shyly. "Do you really think I did well?"

"I think you have experienced some personal growth, Sir, which is always a positive development."

I munched my toast thoughtfully. "I have a new mission, Bentley. I'm going to go in for personal growth in a big way."

"Shall I acquire some books on the subject, Sir?"

"Oh no, the old bean couldn't take it. No reading, I'm afraid."

"I could hire some tutors on philosophy."

"Heavens no! That sounds gruesome! No, I'm sure I can figure it out for myself. I'll just sit here and eat toast and stare into the fire and... think."

He stood for a long moment, watching me. "Are you thinking now, Sir?"

"As a matter of fact, I am."

"About personal growth?"

"About eggs. I am determined to acquire some. Imagine what Cook could accomplish with them."

"You must first acquire some chickens, Sir. There are rumors of sightings in some of the more distant provinces."

"Why chickens?"

"It is chickens that lay the eggs."

"But if we begin with eggs, they will invariably hatch into chickens."

"I believe the chickens must come first, Sir."

"I am certain it will be easier to begin with eggs."

"Chickens, Sir."

"Eggs, Bentley."

"You seem to have strong convictions on the chicken-egg controversy so I shall withdraw. Good night, Sir."

"Yes, good night."

He misted off. A fine fellow, Bentley, but obviously no farmer. This required scientific thinking, which was Ernie's bailiwick. Tomorrow I'd have him drop everything and concentrate on egg production. It seemed I had a flair for business after all. Perhaps it was time I took control of my various industries and ran them myself. Imagine how pleased my relatives would be at the huge increase in profits that would undoubtedly result. I took a large bite of toast, settled back in my chair and promptly fell fast asleep.

THE END

I hope you had as much fun reading about my adventure as I did living it.
If you wish Bentley's chronicles to continue to thrive, I beg you to tell the world by leaving a review!
Click or follow this impossibly opaque link:
https://www.amazon.com/dp/B0B4HP25LT

If you'd like advance notice on the next book's release head to:
WWW.TwitsChronicles.com
where you can sign up for Bentley's email list and where you can ask me or anyone of my acquaintance a question which may be answered in the next newsletter.
I'm told that spam is detestable and so will keep emails to a minimum.

Cyril, Bentley and The Usual Suspects will return in:

TWITS ABROAD

Read on for a taste:

I don't know if you've heard of this Isaac Newton chap, but apparently, he had brains positively leaking out of his ears. He said something to the effect that for everything pleasant that happens, there will be something equally beastly lurking around the corner. This is the only scientific fact I have retained from my school days, and time has proven it true. There I was, happily downing Cook's warm scones with cherry preserves and washing them down with the old lapsang souchong when Bentley slid in with the news that my Aunt Hypatia was chewing the furniture in the parlour and demanding to see me. Bentley, if you are meeting him for the first time, is a steam-powered domestic with a stately dome and an air of moral certainty that will brook no opposition.

"What does my aunt want? Did she say?"

"She did not, although I was able to discern the phrases, 'young pup' and 'cease this shilly-shallying' from amidst the general verbiage."

"This bodes ill. You couldn't tell her I have appendicitis?"

"I could not."

Experience has taught me that making my aunt wait only allows the venom to accumulate in her fangs. I sighed and took a final bite of scone. "May as well take the ball by the horns, what?"

Bentley raised an eyebrow. "Bull, Sir."

"Pardon?"

"One takes the bull by the horns. Balls do not typically have horns."

I thought this over for a tick. "What's a bull?"

"A bull was a male cow, Sir."

"Damn the Great Extinction!"

Bentley assumed a professorial tone. "It was also used to refer to the male of several other extinct species, including elephants."

That perked me up. I love being able to spread out what few nuggets of scholarly wisdom I possess for all and sundry to admire. "I am acquainted with elephants. They were known for holding grudges."

He tilted his head. "For remembering, Sir. I don't believe there was any malice involved."

"Then my aunt is certainly not an elephant. Her memory is used exclusively for mischief."

Bentley gave a little sigh. "We're rather losing the thread."

"It was you that brought up elephants."

"I apologize most abjectly. It was entirely my fault."

"You're being too hard on yourself as usual, Bentley. Well, let's see what the old girl wants."

My Aunt Hypatia could be called a dragon in that her scaly exterior was impervious to attack and that she breathed fire when aroused. Bentley's intelligence had led me to expect a certain Visigoth flavour in my aunt's demeanor so I was surprised to find her smiling at me as if I were a shining example of natural selection.

"Good morning, Aunt. Confusion to our enemies."

"Cyril, darling! Is that the new motto?"

"According to Bentley."

"I think he can be trusted. Confusion to our enemies. Let me look at you."

I was happy to oblige as it required no effort from me. After regarding me up and down, the bottom of her face formed a smile while the upper half held a private meeting to discuss its findings.

"You look tired. Are you getting enough sleep?"

"Oodles. I'm really making an effort!"

"You've lost weight. Do you still employ that eccentric cook of yours?"

"I've gained three pounds and it was worth every mouthful thanks to what you call my 'eccentric cook.'"

"And that mechanical servant of yours—don't you find these older models require endless amounts of maintenance?"

The alarm bells began clanging in my noggin. She clearly had an agenda, and that was bound to be hard luck for me.

"Bentley does his own maintenance."

She pursed her lips judiciously. "I have thought for some time that Bentley is not a good influence on you."

A cold sweat began to gather on the nape of my neck. "Bentley is indispensable. I would sooner part with my thumbs than Bentley."

My aunt waved away my objections. "Well, thumbs are over-rated anyway. A gentleman should use his thumbs as little as possible. That is what servants are for."

"He practically raised me, after all."

"That is no recommendation. His code made it impossible for him to discipline you and because he himself is a mechanism he was incapable of teaching you how humans actually behave. Consequently you are like a dog that is raised to believe it is a person and views other dogs with amused condescension. No, I'm afraid that cannot be counted among Bentley's accomplishments."

I desperately tried to shunt her off onto a side track.

"How's Uncle Hugo? I trust you left him well?"

"I left him adding and subtracting in his little office. He can do no harm in there and will emerge exhausted, which is ideal. A well-rested husband is the Devil's plaything. You should take up some enervating hobbies yourself."

It was high time to take the ball by the horns. Sorry... bull. "Look here, Aunt, why this sudden interest in my domestic affairs?"

"It seems to me that this higgledy-piggledy bachelor life you lead is taking a terrible toll on you. I am naturally concerned."

"And I suppose your remedy is to attach some weak-eyed barnacle like Euphonia Gumboot to me in matrimony?"

My aunt glared down her nose at me. "Euphonia Gumboot is the daughter of my oldest friend. I consider that recommendation enough. If you feel any sense of obligation for the affection I have lavished on you since childhood, you will oblige me by marrying her at once."

"I don't like her."

She smiled with satisfaction. "You see? It's as if you've been married for years. She will take you in hand."

"I don't want to be taken in hand. I'm quite happy as I am."

"You are not. No man who possesses youth, money and freedom can be happy until those things are taken away by a loving partner. We never appreciate a thing until it is gone. It is like the pang one feels upon eating the last chocolate in the box—even inferior chocolate leaves one with a certain wistfulness."

"Euphonia Gumboot is a blight and a pestilence."

"She is waiting in the car."

TWITS was originally produced and distributed by Dori Berinstein, Alan Seales and the Broadway Podcast Network - the premier digital storytelling destination for everyone, everywhere who loves theatre and the performing arts. You can hear an audio play based on Twits in Love performed by an all-star cast including Michael Urie, Christian Borle, Mary Testa and a slew of Broadway luminaries at BPN.fm/Twits

About The Author

Born in Canton Ohio and raised in a box made out of ticky-tacky, Tom Alan Robbins spent his youth as a middle-aged character actor. He has appeared in nine Broadway shows, including *The Lion King* in which he created the role of Pumbaa. He recently received a Grammy nomination for the cast album of *Little Shop of Horrors*. He has maintained a parallel career as a writer, penning scripts for TV shows like *Coach* and writing plays, one of which (*Muse*) recently won the New Works of Merit Playwriting Competition.

The Twits Chronicles series is his first attempt at novel writing and it has been a pure joy. He hopes to keep creating adventures for Cyril and

Bentley as long as there are readers who enjoy them.

Also By Tom Alan Robbins